**"I want this to wo** **Ryan."**

"Do you?"

Marsha bristled but held her tongue.

"Or are you hoping I'll make mistakes, so Ryan will want nothing to do with me?"

"I can't believe you'd think that."

"Why not? If things don't work out for me and Ryan, you head back to California with a clear conscience."

The brown eyes staring at her were filled with pain, and shame swept through Marsha. She expected that this father-son reunion would be difficult, but her main concern had been for Ryan's emotional well-being. She hadn't given much thought to the turmoil Will might be dealing with. "I'll do everything in my power to help you both, but you'll have to communicate with me. I can't read your mind."

Will stared into space. "We're strangers who made a baby."

"Then why don't we get reacquainted," she said.

Dear Reader,

The famous Willie Nelson song "Always on my Mind" was the inspiration for Will and Marsha's story.

Will Cash has never been able to forget the one-night stand he had with the pastor's daughter back in high school, and for good reason—fourteen years later Marsha returns to town with his son, Ryan.

Keeping secrets can lead to big-time trouble and Marsha Bugler is about to discover just what kind of hornet's nest she's stirred up when she informs not only her parents who the father of their grandson is, but the father himself—Will Cash, who had no idea she'd kept their baby.

There's plenty of drama in this story and I hope you enjoy watching Will, Marsha, their son and her parents find their own path toward forgiveness and reconciliation. And through it all the meaning of family shines true and bright.

*Her Secret Cowboy* is the third book in The Cash Brothers series. If you missed the first two stories, *The Cowboy Next Door* (July 1013) and *Twins Under the Christmas Tree* (Oct 2013), the books remain available through online retailers.

For more information on future Cash Brothers books visit www.marinthomas.com. I love to connect with my readers—you'll find me on FB, Twitter and Goodreads, and be sure to check out The Cash Brothers Facebook page as well as their Pinterest boards!

Happy Ever After...The Cowboy Way!

Marin

# HER SECRET COWBOY

—

## Marin Thomas

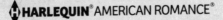

**HARLEQUIN**® AMERICAN ROMANCE®

Recycling programs
for this product may
not exist in your area.

ISBN-13: 978-0-373-75507-3

HER SECRET COWBOY

Copyright © 2014 by Brenda Smith-Beagley

**Printed in U.S.A.**

## ABOUT THE AUTHOR

Marin Thomas grew up in Janesville, Wisconsin. She left the Midwest to attend college in Tucson, Arizona, where she earned a B.A. in radio-TV. Following graduation she married her college sweetheart in a five-minute ceremony at the historic Little Chapel of the West in Las Vegas, Nevada. Over the years she and her family have lived in seven different states, but they've now come full circle and returned to Arizona, where the rugged desert and breathtaking sunsets provide plenty of inspiration for Marin's cowboy books.

### Books by Marin Thomas

**HARLEQUIN AMERICAN ROMANCE**

*The McKade Brothers
**Hearts of Appalachia
***Rodeo Rebels
‡The Cash Brothers

To my new sister-in-law, Tammy O'Day Smith—*"Once in a while, right in the middle of an ordinary life, love gives us a fairy tale."* Wishing you and Brett your very own happy-ever-after fairy tale—Texas-sized.

# Chapter One

Will Cash pulled off the road and parked next to the mailbox at the entrance to the family pecan farm. Lately he'd been the only one who bothered to bring in the mail. Conway should train his twin stepsons to ride their bikes to the box, but maybe five-year-olds were too young for that kind of responsibility.

As usual the box was stuffed. He gathered the envelopes and hopped into the truck, then directed the air vents toward his face. Normal highs for June were in the low nineties but today's temperature hovered near one hundred, promising a long hot summer for southwest Arizona.

Will sifted through the pile. Grocery-store ads, business fliers, electric bill, a statement from Warehouse Furniture—Conway and his new wife, Isi, were remodeling the farmhouse. A boot catalog for Merle Haggard Cash—otherwise known as Mack to friends and family. His younger brother spent way too much money on fancy footwear, but he liked to look sharp when his band, Cowboy Rebels, played at the local honky-tonks. His fingers froze on a letter addressed to Willie Nelson Cash. He didn't recognize the feminine script and there was no return address. Before he examined the envelope further, his cell phone rang.

"Hold your horses, Porter. I'll be there in a minute." Wednesday night was poker night and his brothers and brother-in-law were waiting for him in the bunkhouse. If not for the weekly card game, they'd hardly see each other.

His sister, Dixie, and her husband, Gavin, lived in Yuma—forty-five minutes away. Will's eldest brother, Johnny, had married his boss's daughter, and he and Shannon lived in the foreman's cabin at the Triple D Ranch. And Mack spent most of the week and every other weekend as a trail hand at the Black Jack Mountain Dude Ranch. That left Will, Buck and Porter living in the bunkhouse on the farm.

He tossed the mail aside and drove on—slowly. The days of racing along the dirt road had ended when Conway married Isi and they moved into the farmhouse with the twins and a black Lab named Bandit. He parked in the yard and as soon as he got out of the pickup, his nephews ambushed him.

"Uncle Will, guess what we made?"

Will walked up to the porch where the boys sat on the steps with the dog wedged between them. The twins wore blue jeans and identical Western shirts in different colors—Javier liked red and Miguel preferred blue. "What are you guys up to?"

Miguel held out a piece of paper. "It's Bandit's new doghouse."

Will examined the crude drawing. "Who's gonna build it?"

"Our dad said you could build Bandit a house."

*Of course he did.* Will worked in construction, so

naturally he was the go-to guy in the family for projects involving a hammer and nails.

"We can help." Javier's big brown eyes pleaded with Will.

"Okay, I'll build Bandit a house, but you'll have to wait awhile." Will worked for a family-owned construction company run by Ben Wallace—a guy he'd gone to high school with. Ben had landed a new job to construct a classroom wing on the Mission Community Church. The work would keep them busy for weeks.

"I'll give your dad a list of supplies to buy at the lumberyard," Will said.

The boys raced down the porch steps and threw their arms around his legs. "Thanks, Uncle Will," Miguel said.

"You're welcome. Now go inside."

Javier shook his head. "We have to stay out here 'cause baby Nate's sleeping."

While the men played cards the women sat in the house and did whatever it was that married women did—probably talk about their husbands. "Don't get into trouble." Will walked over to the bunkhouse, opening the letter addressed to him. When he removed the note inside, a photo fell out and landed on his steel-toed boot. He snatched it off the ground and stared at the teenage boy.

*What the heck?*

*Dear Will...* He read a few more lines but the words blurred and a loud buzzing filled his ears. The kid in the picture was named Ryan and he was fourteen years old.

Slowly Will's eyes focused and he studied the photo. The young man had the same brownish-blond hair as

Will's but his eyes weren't brown—they were blue like his mother's.

"Buck!" he shouted. "Get your ass out here right now!"

The farmhouse door opened and his sister stepped outside. "Willie Nelson Cash, don't you dare swear in front of the boys."

"Take the twins inside, Dixie." She must have sensed his dark mood, because she did as he asked without mouthing off. Will stared at the bunkhouse, afraid if he went inside he'd tear the place apart. When Buck came out, the rest of the Cash brothers and their brother-in-law, Gavin, followed.

"What's wrong?" Johnny's blue eyes darkened with concern.

Will ignored his eldest brother—if Johnny had his way he'd take control of the situation like he'd done all through their childhood. This was Will's fight with Buck and no one else's.

"What's got you fired up?" Porter ran a hand through his shaggy hair and flashed his boyish grin—the one that stopped women from one to ninety-nine in their tracks. "Steam's spewing from your ears."

"Shut up, Porter." Will glared at his younger brother. "This is between me and Buck."

"I've never seen you this pissed." Conway glanced at his brothers. "Maybe you ought to take a couple of deep breaths before you go off half-cocked."

"Is that what you tell the twins when they're itching for a fight?" Now that the handsomest Cash brother had settled down and become a father, he liked to believe he was the mature one.

"Conway's right." Mack's deep baritone voice carried over the heads of his brothers. "Whatever's got you riled, Will, it's not like you to attack one of us."

What Mack said was true, but Will had never been in a pickle like this before. His musician brother could write a song about the news he'd just received and make a fortune off Will's misery.

"This concerns Buck and me." Will shook the letter. "You knew all along."

Buck stepped forward, using his broad shoulders to push his brothers out of the way. "Knew what?" Of all his siblings, Buck was the quietest and through the years he'd assumed the role of family peacemaker. Too bad this was one dispute he wouldn't be able to settle to Will's satisfaction.

"Remember Marsha Bugler?"

"Of course. Why?"

"She said you'd vouch for her that she's telling the truth."

His brother's eye twitched—a sure sign of guilt. "The truth about what?"

"That after I got her pregnant, she kept the baby."

The color drained from Buck's face.

The tenuous hold Will had on his temper broke, and he let Buck have it. "You've kept in touch with Marsha since high school. How the hell could you not tell me that I had a son!"

Buck's pleading gaze swung to Johnny. "Honest to God, I didn't know Ryan was Will's son until a short while ago."

"What do you mean by that?" Will's intestines twisted into a giant knot.

"Marsha didn't tell me you were Ryan's father until I saw her in March."

"This past March?"

"A year ago March," Buck muttered.

Will lunged for Buck, but Johnny held him tight. "You knew I had a son for over a year!"

"She made me promise not to spill the beans until she had a chance to tell you," Buck said.

"To heck with promising Marsha, I'm your brother." Will's chest physically ached at the thought of his own flesh and blood keeping the truth from him.

"Marsha never planned to tell me at first, but I confronted her when I noticed Ryan looked like you."

Will wasn't buying his brother's story. "It took you thirteen years to make the connection between me and Ryan?"

"I only looked up Marsha a few times since she'd moved to Los Angeles and Ryan was never there when I stopped by until…March."

"How good of friends are you with Marsha? Have you slept with her?"

"It's not like that between us, Will."

Will had known the answer before he'd asked the question, but he was desperate to find a way out of this mess. "Is there a chance Ryan isn't my kid?"

"Marsha's not a slut." Buck jabbed his finger in the air.

"If she had sex with me on the first date there's no telling who she slept with before she went off to college."

Buck jumped forward, his fist clipping Will across the jaw. Will stumbled, then regained his balance and threw a punch that connected with Buck's cheek. His brothers attempted to intervene, but Will was too angry to care who he hit. He shoved Mack out of the way then took aim again, but Buck ducked and Will's fist smashed into Porter's face.

"Shit, Will! I think you broke my nose!" Porter held his face in his hands and moaned.

Johnny stepped forward and punched Will in the stomach. Will dropped to his knees and wheezed. "Are you going to behave or do I need to tie you down?"

His brother would carry through with his threat. When they were kids, they'd gotten into an argument and Johnny had tied Will's hands to the porch post with a piece of rope then took off. Will had waited three hours for Grandma Ada and Dixie to come home and free him.

"Everyone get in the bunkhouse." Johnny scowled at the brothers until they obeyed.

After the yard emptied out, Johnny said, "Let's go."

Will followed his brother, because he didn't know what else to do. He'd never felt so lost, helpless or angry.

They hiked in silence until the family graveyard came into view. Johnny sat beneath the ancient pecan tree, which shaded the tombstones. Unable to articulate his thoughts and feelings Will paced in front of the ornate gate surrounding the plots.

"You're about to explode. Let it out."

"Look at me." Will spread his arms wide. "I've got no business being a father."

"Whether you do or don't doesn't matter. The deed is done."

"I've got nothing to show my son. I'm a grown man who lives in a bunkhouse with his brothers. I drive a thirteen-year-old vehicle and the most expensive thing I own is my rodeo gear and my truck."

"Don't sell yourself short. You've got plenty to offer."

"Yeah? Like what?"

"Like being a father to your son. That's more than you grew up with."

Johnny's words sent a cold chill through Will.

"Did Marsha give a reason why she waited until now to contact you about Ryan?"

"No. I don't have a clue why she suddenly wants to come clean with me."

"Then she owes you some answers," Johnny said.

"How am I supposed to look my son in the eye after I insisted his mother get rid of him?"

"Maybe Marsha hasn't told Ryan the circumstances of his birth," Johnny said.

"And if she did? Then what?"

Johnny shrugged. "You cross that bridge when you come to it."

"Damn." Will punched the air with his fist. "Ben signed a contract to work on the Mission Community Church." And the church's pastor was Jim Bugler— Marsha's father. Ryan's grandfather. "I can't face the pastor after I abandoned his grandson."

"You can't abandon a person you didn't know existed."

"You're wrong, Johnny. I deserted Ryan when I told Marsha I didn't want to be a father." There was no getting past that fact.

"Give yourself time to get used to the idea."

"No chance of that happening. Marsha and Ryan are spending the summer in Stagecoach."

"When does she plan to arrive?"

"Tomorrow."

In less than twenty-four hours Will would head down a path he'd never planned to travel.

"How come we're staying the whole summer at Grandpa and Grandma's?"

Marsha took her eyes off the road for a second and glanced at her son. "Because they're getting older and they won't be here forever." The forever part might come sooner rather than later for her father.

Right after Christmas her mother had phoned with the news that her father's prostate cancer had taken a turn for the worse. The most worrisome news had been learning he'd refused all further treatment except hormone therapy. At seventy-nine, she understood his reluctance to endure a second round of radiation and more surgery. Marsha hadn't told Ryan the seriousness of his grandfather's health, because her parents had asked her not to.

The day she'd first learned of her father's cancer diagnosis she'd been in a state of panic and then Buck had shown up on her doorstep. He'd been in town for a rodeo and hadn't called ahead to tell her he was stopping by. That morning Ryan had been home. Buck had taken one look at her thirteen-year-old son and recognized the resemblance to his brother.

Marsha's secret was out.

After Ryan left the apartment to go to a friend's house, Buck asked if Will was Ryan's father and Marsha had told him the truth. Buck had been stunned and angry that she'd kept Ryan a secret all these years but Marsha had begged him not to tell Will. She'd confessed that she was having difficulty dealing with her father's cancer diagnosis and feared revealing the identity of her son's father right now would overwhelm Ryan. Buck had reluctantly agreed to keep her secret.

One month had turned into two then three and before she knew it, a year had passed since Buck's visit and she still hadn't found the courage to contact Will. The news that her father had stopped fighting his cancer had forced Marsha to confront the past head-on.

Marsha understood the risks in coming clean with Will after she'd gone against his wishes to keep their child. He'd been adamant that he wasn't ready to be a father. And she hadn't been ready to be a mother, but the conscience of a pastor's daughter refused to allow her to abort a baby or let her father go to his grave without knowing who'd gotten her pregnant.

Ryan turned the page on his Kindle, then asked, "What are you gonna do all summer?"

"I'm working as an online tutor for the University of Southern California," she reminded him. Marsha taught high-school chemistry and had completed her doctoral degree a year ago and hoped to work her way into a teaching position at a university.

"Does Grandma still have her library card?"

"I'm sure she does." Her mother paid extra for a membership to the Yuma County Library so Ryan had plenty of reading material to keep him entertained. In exchange for the use of the library card, Ryan helped his grandmother in the church garden.

Even though she'd taken precautions by never telling Buck when she was in town and avoiding cowboy hangouts and local rodeos, Marsha was surprised that she'd managed to avoid running into Will or his siblings during her two-week visits home.

She slowed the car as it approached the four-way stop in Stagecoach. The town was comprised of a handful of businesses, their brick exteriors faded by the desert sun. The main drag consisted of bars, Vern's Drive-

In, the Pawn Palace, Mel's Barber Shop, the Bee Luv Lee Beauty Salon, where Marsha's former high-school friend worked, José's Mexican Diner, a Chevron gas station and a Wells Fargo Savings and Loan.

"Not much has changed since last summer," she said.

Ryan grunted, but didn't glance up from his e-reader.

She hoped she wasn't making a huge mistake introducing Ryan to his father. Unlike her son, Will hadn't cared much about school or grades. She worried that instead of seeing all the special qualities Ryan possessed, Will would find him lacking.

"Can we go to the library tomorrow?" Ryan asked.

"I've got plans."

"What are you doing?"

"Meeting an old friend of mine."

"Who?"

"A boy I went to high school with." She turned onto the gravel road that led to the Mission Community Church. A quarter mile later she parked in front of her parents' stucco ranch house, which sat fifty yards from the church. "Grandma's waiting at the door."

Marsha turned off the car, and they both got out. "Leave the luggage for now."

"Look at you, Ryan," Sara Bugler exclaimed. "You've grown at least two inches since you were here last."

Ryan hugged his grandmother. "I'm taller than Mom now."

"Yes, you are."

"You look good, Mom." They exchanged hugs. "Where's Dad?"

"He fell asleep on the patio." Her mother led the way through the house. "Jim, Marsha and Ryan are here."

His face gaunt, her father sat in a lounge chair with

the newspaper folded in his lap. She held his hands and kissed his cheek. "How are you, Dad?"

"Fine, daughter." His eyes sparkled when he held his arms out to Ryan.

Marsha's throat tightened as she watched the two men in her life hug.

"I've got a new word game we can play, Grandpa," Ryan said.

"Good. I was getting tired of beating you at the old one."

No matter what happened between her and Will, Marsha refused to regret spending the next two and a half months with her parents.

"Come in the house, dear." Marsha followed her mother inside while Ryan remained with his grandfather. "What can I get you to drink?"

"Iced tea if you have it," Marsha said.

Her mother poured two glasses of tea and sat at the kitchen table. After a brief conversation on how Ryan had done in school this past semester and Marsha's tutoring job, her mother said, "You haven't spent an entire summer here since you graduated from high school."

"I don't know how fast Dad's cancer is going to progress and I..." She blinked back tears. "I want him and Ryan to have as much time together as possible."

"I'm not sure it's a good idea for you two to stay so long."

"Why? Are you concerned we might be too taxing on Dad?"

"No, your father is thrilled you're here."

"Then what are you worried about?"

Her mother stared at the wall instead of answering.

"You're acting weird, Mom. What's going on?"

"Did I tell you that the church is getting a new classroom wing built this summer?"

"You did. What does that have to do with me and Ryan?"

"Ben Wallace's construction company won the bid."

Marsha had gone to school with Ben. "And that's important because…?"

"Will Cash works for Ben."

*Oh, God. She knows.* "Does Dad…"

Her mother sighed. "Don't think for a minute I haven't beaten myself up over the years and had many heart-to-heart talks with the Lord about keeping your secret."

"Why haven't you told Dad?"

"I worry how he'll take the news."

"I was planning to introduce Ryan to Will this visit." Her mother gasped and Marsha held up her hand. "Hear me out. Dad's the only male role model in Ryan's life right now. If—" *when* "—something happens to Dad, Ryan's going to need a man to lean on."

"Will Cash isn't a suitable role model for Ryan."

This was why Marsha had never told her parents who'd fathered Ryan. As much as Sara and Jim Bugler were God-fearing people and had raised her to show empathy and compassion for the less fortunate, Marsha had grown up hearing her parents' occasional comments about Will's promiscuous mother, Aimee Cash, and the wild band of ruffians she handed over to her parents to raise while she gallivanted through the state sleeping with men.

"I won't know if Will is a suitable role model until he has a chance to show me," Marsha said.

"Ryan could get hurt. He's nothing like those Cash boys."

"The Cash brothers aren't wild teenagers anymore—they're grown men." She closed her eyes and counted to ten. "Mom, I'm asking you to please not speak badly of Will. If he wants Ryan to know about the skeletons in the Cash family closet, he should be the one to tell him."

"When is Ryan meeting Will?"

"Tomorrow."

"You've told Ryan about his father then?"

"Not yet." She'd chickened out.

Her mother took their empty glasses to the sink. "It certainly won't be a dull summer."

No, it wouldn't. Marsha had a feeling it was going to be three months of fireworks—explosions she hoped didn't all blow up in her face.

## *Chapter Two*

Will sat on the sofa in the bunkhouse and waited for Marsha to arrive. He'd gotten home from work an hour ago and had showered and dressed in clean clothes. His chest felt as if a fifty-pound anvil rested on his rib cage and drawing air into his lungs took major effort.

He glanced at his watch. She was late.

Marsha had texted him last night, asking to meet alone this afternoon. At first he'd been puzzled, wondering how she'd gotten his number, then realized all she'd had to do was ask her father. Both Ben and Will's cell numbers were on the construction contract with the church.

"You're going to burn a hole in that wall if you stare at it any harder," Buck said.

Will studied his brother who sat at the table drinking coffee. "I thought you were working today." This was the first exchange he'd had with Buck since their confrontation over Marsha's letter.

"Troy took off early to drive to Tucson for a car show."

"Heck of a way to run a business."

Buck carried his mug to the sink. "One day I'll start my own auto-repair shop."

"You've been saying that for the past two years." Porter flipped through the pages of an *American Cowboy* magazine.

"You don't have a job right now so you don't get to comment." Buck swatted Porter upside the head.

"Hey, don't mess with the hair." Porter smoothed his hand over his golden-brown locks. "Rodeo is a job."

"It's employment only when you win, which you don't do often," Buck said.

Will went back to staring at the wall. Not even his brothers' bickering distracted him from the feeling of impending doom that had nagged him since Marsha's text.

"Mack's too busy at the dude ranch to rodeo on weekends," Porter said. "I need a new roping partner." He tore a page from the magazine, wadded it into a ball and threw it at Will, pinging him in the shoulder. "Want to team rope with me this Saturday at the Midway Rodeo?"

Will didn't rodeo much anymore, because he often ended up working seven days a week to finish a construction job. "What about horses?"

"Greg Patterson said he'd bring an extra pair if we give him a cut of the winnings."

"You that confident we're gonna win?" Will asked.
Porter chuckled. "No."

"Count me in." Will needed an outlet for his anxiety.

The rumble of a car engine drifted through the bunkhouse walls and Will bolted to the window. A red Honda SUV pulled into the yard.

"Let me see." Porter pushed his way between Buck and Will. "When did she get boobs?"

Will gaped at the woman who stepped from the car.

This was *not* the Marsha Bugler he'd taken to the prom his senior year.

"Show some respect, Porter." Buck elbowed his brother. "She's the pastor's daughter."

Will soaked in the sight of his son's mother. Marsha was tall, and the tight, faded jeans and fancy cowgirl boots emphasized her long legs. Shoot, he couldn't recall what shoes she'd worn to the prom, never mind the color of her dress. Golden curls fell over her shoulders and the black V-neck T-shirt showed off her generous breasts. The curls were familiar but not the boobs—their groping in the pickup had been done with most of their clothes on.

"They might be fake," Porter said.

Marsha stumbled when she walked up the porch steps. The way her breasts jiggled settled the matter—they were real.

"I heard that some women go through a second puberty and—"

"Get lost, Porter," Will said.

Isi had taken the boys into town earlier and there was no one to answer Marsha's knock on the farmhouse door. She shielded her eyes against the afternoon sun and stared in the direction of the bunkhouse.

"Aren't you going to go out there?" Buck asked.

"I'm going." Will stepped outside, slamming the door behind him. The noise drew Marsha's attention and for the first time in over fourteen years they made eye contact.

Aware Buck and Porter spied through the window and Conway stood in the barn watching, Will ignored the urge to flee and met Marsha in the middle of the yard.

"Hello, Will."

Her voice rang with confidence and the directness of her gaze knocked him off balance. The woman standing before him was nothing like the high school girl who'd barely conversed with him. "Marsha."

"Thank you for agreeing to meet with me."

It wasn't every day a man found out he was a father. Did she have any idea how her letter had turned his life upside down? Her expression remained neutral, but she clenched and unclenched her hands. She was more nervous than she let on. *Good. She should be.*

"I'm sure you have questions," she said.

"A few."

She squared her shoulders. He hadn't remembered her being spirited—only shy and studious. She'd been the complete opposite of the girls he'd chased in school. The wild girls had been the only ones willing to date a guy like him.

"If you expect me to apologize—" her eyes blazed "—I'm not going to."

She might as well have slapped him across the face with her stinging statement. Of course the pastor's daughter considered herself above needing forgiveness.

"I had my reasons, Will, whether they were right or wrong, they were mine and I don't regret keeping Ryan. Nothing you say or do can make me feel guilty for not aborting my son."

"Your son?"

A pink blush spread across her cheeks. "Our son."

"What about hiding Ryan from me? Feel any guilt over that?"

She lowered her gaze. "Is there somewhere we can talk in private?"

"The front porch." Away from his brothers' prying

eyes. They walked past the house in silence, the intermittent breeze carrying the scent of Marsha's perfume beneath Will's nose—a light, citrusy smell that made him want to take off her clothes. He ground his teeth and silently cursed himself for finding her attractive.

When they reached the front yard, he spoke. "Why did you suddenly decide to tell me about Ryan?" He doubted her reason had to do with guilt, otherwise she'd have come forward years ago.

"My father's ill."

Stagecoach was a small town. Will's boss happened to be a member of the Community Mission Church and had told him about the pastor's health issues. "What does your father's prostate cancer have to do with being truthful with me?"

"Ryan's very close to his grandfather and when he's gone…" She cleared her throat. "Ryan won't have a man to look up to."

Will was the last person on earth who should be a role model. Feeling as if Marsha had backed him into a corner, he lashed out—more from fear than anger. "Would you have ever told me about Ryan if your father hadn't become ill?"

She stared him in the eye, which wasn't difficult considering she was at least five feet ten inches in her boots and he was six feet in his boots. "You told me to get an abortion. You said under no circumstances did you want to be a father."

"I was eighteen, Marsha." He paced in front of her. "That's what a typical eighteen-year-old guy tells the girl he got pregnant." He hadn't suggested giving the baby up for adoption because he was afraid he'd be just like his old man.

"I was eighteen, too. Old enough to make up my own mind about whether or not I was ready to be a mother."

She'd avoided answering his question, so he answered it for her. "You wouldn't have told me about Ryan if your father hadn't become ill."

"I would have told you…eventually."

"You're a liar. Buck forced your hand." When she didn't respond, Will said, "My brother should have told me right away when he found out."

"I'm not here to talk about what Buck should or shouldn't have done. I was prepared to tell Ryan about you years ago, but he didn't show any interest in learning who his father was."

"None at all?" The question escaped his mouth in a choked whisper.

She shook her head.

Stunned, Will closed his eyes as a memory better left buried resurrected itself. When he'd turned twelve, he'd wanted to know more about his father and had pestered his mother for information. She'd brushed off Will's questions, but he'd badgered her until one afternoon she'd dragged him by the shirt collar to the car and drove him to Tucson.

She never said a word the entire trip until she stopped in front of a single-story home with toys strewn across the yard.

"Your father lives in that house."

"What's his name?"

"Henry Blythe."

"Can I ring the doorbell?" he'd asked.

"It's up to you."

Will was cocky enough to believe he could handle anything, so he strolled up to the house and rang the bell. A woman answered the door and two little kids poked their heads out from behind her legs. "Is Mr. Blythe home?" Will asked.

"Yes, who are you?"

"Willie Cash, ma'am."

"Wait here." She shut the door in his face. He stood on the porch so long his legs became tired and he sat on the stoop. His mother waited with him—never leaving the car. After an hour Will rang the doorbell again. And again. And again. The sun set. And he waited. And waited. And waited.

Finally the door opened.

A man stood in the shadows. Will couldn't make out his features, but his voice sounded hoarse and mean. "Go away, kid."

Shaking in his shoes, Will asked, "Are you my father?"

"With a mother like yours, you're not good enough to be anyone's kid." The door slammed in his face.

From that day forward Will hadn't given Henry Blythe a second thought, but deep down the man's rejection had left its mark. Will accepted that he was no good because of who his mother was—a woman who'd borne seven children—six of them fathered by different men. That Ryan had never been interested in knowing Will reminded him of the shame he carried.

Feeling like a cornered animal Will lashed out, "What do you want from me?"

Marsha backpedaled. "If you don't want to meet your son, say so and we won't interfere in your life."

"It's easy to paint me the bad guy, isn't it?" He pointed his finger. "You want everything on your terms and you expect me to be grateful that you're allowing me to see my son."

"You don't know what it was like to be in my shoes—eighteen, pregnant and…" She rubbed her temples as if she had a headache. "I didn't come here to argue with you. Go ahead and hate me. I don't care."

Will might have believed her if her voice hadn't cracked.

"What matters now is doing what's best for Ryan," she said.

Damn, he admired her spunk. To his knowledge his mother had never stood up to any of his siblings' fathers the way Marsha stood up to Will. Maybe the outcome of his confrontation with Henry Blythe would have been different if his mother had accompanied him to the door that afternoon.

"Do you want to meet your son or not?"

"Of course." The words sounded sure, but deep down Will was terrified.

"When?"

"There's a rodeo in Midway on Saturday. I told Porter I'd team rope with him. You and Ryan could meet us there."

"What time?"

"One o'clock," he said.

"Fine."

"Are you going to tell Ryan about me before Saturday?"

"Yes."

He'd like to be a fly on the wall during that conversation. "What have your parents got to say about all this?"

"I didn't tell them you were Ryan's father."

Now he knew why the pastor had never shown up at

the pecan farm with a shotgun, demanding he do right by his daughter.

"My mother suspected it was you a while ago." The corner of her mouth curved upward. "Ryan looks like you."

Her words barely registered with Will as he stared at her mouth. Blame it on his confused emotional state but right now all he wanted to do was taste Marsha's kiss. Why he'd want to kiss the woman who'd betrayed him was a mystery, but there was no denying her presence was causing a spike in his testosterone levels.

"Are you okay?" She frowned.

"I'm fine." *Pull it together, man.* "Your mother didn't share her suspicions with your father?"

"No."

He didn't envy Marsha the task of breaking the news to the pastor—the man had never held the Cash family in high esteem. Working at the church next week would prove interesting.

When they walked to Marsha's car, Will said, "In case no one told you…I work for Ben Wallace's construction company and we're—"

"I heard." She opened the driver-side door. "I'm sorry if I came off… I didn't mean to be…" She nibbled her lip. "I'm worried about my father."

Unlike Will, Marsha had a good relationship with her parents and he sympathized with her having to deal with the pastor's illness. "See you Saturday," he said. Her car had no sooner disappeared from sight than all three of his brothers appeared at Will's side.

"Well?" Conway said. "Are you positive you're Ryan's father?"

"Yes."

"What are you going to do?" Porter asked.

"Marsha's bringing him to the rodeo on Saturday."

"Want me to tag along?" Buck asked.

"No, thanks." The last thing he needed was to over-whelm Ryan with all his uncles. "Porter, we're taking separate vehicles. I'll meet you in Midway."

"Whatever works best for you." Porter nodded to-ward his truck. "Buck and I are heading into Yuma to grocery shop. You got any requests?"

Will shook his head. Once his brothers peeled out of the yard, Conway spoke. "You okay?"

"I don't know the first thing about being a father."

"I didn't either," Conway said.

"How'd you figure it out?"

"You learn as you go."

That sounded risky.

"My advice is to not push yourself on Ryan. Let him call the shots."

"Sounds easy enough."

"It's not. And as soon as you think you understand your kid, they do something that takes you by surprise." Conway retreated to the barn, leaving Will alone with his misgivings.

"RYAN, LET'S TAKE a walk," Marsha said after supper. Her father had retreated to the living room to nap in his recliner and her mother was pulling weeds in the garden.

"I don't want to take a walk. I'm reading the *Land of Varagon*." Ryan had gotten hooked on a new fantasy series after one of the kids in his after-school book club recommended it. There were twelve stories in the series and Ryan was reading number six. She'd kept track of the characters and plots through the fourth book, then things had become confusing and she'd given up.

"I need to talk to you. It's important." She waited by the door.

Ryan set his e-reader on the kitchen table and they walked through the garage then along the path that led to the church.

"How do you feel about meeting your father this summer?" When Ryan remained silent, she said, "You've never asked about him."

"I didn't ask, because I thought you didn't want me to know who he was."

Shocked, she put the brakes on. "Why would you think I wouldn't want you to know who your father was?"

"You never talked about him and he never came to our house." Ryan shrugged. "I thought he was a bad person."

Dear God what had she done? "I'm sorry, Ryan. I assumed your silence meant you weren't interested in getting to know him." As soon as she said the words, a sharp pain struck her in the chest—guilt. How dare she lay the blame at Ryan's feet when her reluctance to include Will in their lives had to do with her own insecurities and nothing to do with wanting to prevent Will from hurting Ryan.

"It's not a big deal, Mom. Lots of kids in my school have only one parent."

"Since we're spending the entire summer with Grandpa and Grandma I thought you should know that your father lives in Stagecoach."

"Really?"

"Yes."

"How come he never wanted to see me when we came to Grandma and Grandpa's?"

"Your father didn't know you existed until recently."

Her throat tightened as she envisioned the wary look on Will's face when they'd met today. It was clear her decision to keep Ryan a secret had wounded him deeply. Then she reminded herself that over a decade had passed since she'd revealed her pregnancy to him and his reaction then had been very different.

"Why didn't you want him to know about me?" Ryan asked.

"I didn't think he was ready to be a father. We'd both just graduated from high school."

"Does he want to meet me or are you forcing him to?"

"Of course he wants to meet you. He'd like for you and I to go to a rodeo and watch him compete this Saturday."

"I don't like rodeos."

"Since when?"

"Since Grandma and Grandpa took me to one when I was six."

"I'd forgotten about that." When Ryan had returned from the event all he'd told her was that it was too noisy and the place stunk like poop.

They arrived at the church and Ryan held the door open for her. They sat in the pew at the front of the sanctuary.

"Is he any good at rodeo?" Ryan asked.

"I don't know. We'll find out on Saturday."

"Do I have to go?"

"Yes." It would be easy to give in to him, but she held firm.

"Mom? What if I don't like him?"

Marsha smiled—she'd always been drawn to Will's brooding personality and good looks. He'd been the quintessential bad boy, the kid with a troubled past, and she'd been the sweet daughter of the local pastor who'd believed she could save him.

"Why are you smiling?" Ryan's question ended her trip down memory lane.

"I bumped into your father in the school hallway once. All my books went flying."

"Did he get mad?"

"No, he helped me pick them up." Then the next day when they'd passed in the hall again she'd said "Hi" but Will had looked right through her.

"You're weird, Mom."

"I know." She stared into Ryan's blue eyes—the same blue as hers. His light brown hair and square jaw were all Will. A wavy lock fell across his forehead and she brushed it away even though he didn't like her fussing over him. "Don't mention meeting your dad to Grandpa."

"Grandpa doesn't know who my dad is?"

"No." She'd taught Ryan from an early age to always tell the truth and she was ashamed that she hadn't modeled the same behavior.

"What's his name?"

"Will Cash."

Ryan's eyes grew round. "Is he Buck's brother?"

"Will is Buck's older brother."

"Am I supposed to call him Dad?"

"That's up to you."

"Is he smart?"

Marsha winced. Ryan's high IQ skewed the way he

viewed the world and people. "I've told you before that not all intelligence comes from book learning."

"Did he go to college?"

"I don't know." Marsha didn't think Will had.

"What's his job?"

"He's a construction worker. As a matter of fact, he's helping to build the new addition on Grandpa's church."

Ryan's eyes widened. "I'm going to see him every day?"

"Probably, but he'll be busy working."

"I don't have to help, do I?"

"I hope you'll pitch in if your grandfather or father asks you to." The conversation needed to end, before it spiraled downward. "You're okay then with going to the rodeo?"

"If I have to."

*You have to.*

As they walked to the house, Marsha wondered again if she was doing the right thing in bringing father and son together. Ryan was nothing like Will might envision for a son and Will was nothing like Ryan might envision for a father.

# Chapter Three

"Ladies and gents, welcome to the thirty-fifth annual Midway Rodeo and Stock Show."

Applause filled the outdoor arena that held two thousand people. From the corner of her eye Marsha observed Ryan soaking in the atmosphere. He'd been quiet since they'd arrived at the fairgrounds. He was nervous about meeting his father, but all she could do was offer her silent support and be there for him if he needed her.

"When's he competing?" Ryan asked.

Marsha flipped through the program she'd purchased while the announcer droned on about the history of the rodeo and famous cowboys who'd claimed national titles. "Looks like your father and uncle are up after the barrel racing event." She pointed to the rodeo workers setting out the barrels in the arena.

"Can I see the bulls before he rides?"

Ryan wasn't into girls yet and she teased him. "Don't you want to watch the cowgirls ride?" He rolled his eyes and she laughed. "Let's look for the livestock pens." She wasn't surprised that Ryan found rodeo boring. He wasn't into sports and his only competition experience came from chess-club matches.

As they approached the livestock pens, Marsha plugged her nose. "Whew, it stinks."

"The bulls don't look mean," Ryan said.

"Maybe not now, but once the gate opens, they turn into ruthless bucking machines."

"Rodeo's stupid."

*Oh, boy.* Will would not welcome hearing his son's opinion of the sport. "It's difficult to appreciate things you don't have any experience in."

"Where are the steers they use for team roping?"

She nodded to a barn. "Maybe in there."

Quite a few cowboys had gathered outside the building but Will and Porter weren't in the group. So as not to interfere with Will's concentration, Marsha hadn't planned on father and son meeting until after the Cash brothers competed. "Let's buy a bag of popcorn."

Ten minutes later they found their seats and the announcer's voice boomed over the sound system. "Ladies and gents, we're ready to kick off the team-roping event."

A group of young women dressed in flashy Western clothes and wearing more makeup than a Mary Kay representative stood and cheered. Marsha whispered in Ryan's ear. "Buckle bunnies."

"Buckle what's?"

Most teenage boys drooled over pretty girls in tight T-shirts and skinny jeans, but not Marsha's son. Ryan would rather bury his head in a book than chase after the opposite sex. As a teacher she appreciated his thirst for knowledge, but as a mother she worried he was missing out on the best part of his youth—first crushes and first kisses. "Buckle bunnies are girls who travel the circuit cheering for the cowboys."

"Do they cheer for my dad?"

Surprised Ryan had referred to Will as his father, she said, "I don't know." As Marsha studied the bunny in front of her—painted-on jeans, rhinestone belt and designer boots—a burning sensation exploded inside her chest. After more than a decade, she still found Will attractive and hated the idea of him being with an empty-headed beauty. She knew from experience that some men were intimidated by smart women, but she refused to play the role of a dumb blonde to land a date.

"Next up in the team-roping competition are the Cash brothers—Porter and Will."

Ryan watched his father and uncle mount their horses in the boxes on both sides of the chute holding the steer. "Which one is he?"

Back to *he* again. "Will's the heeler. He's going to toss—"

"Yeah, I know. He ropes the steer's rear legs after the header ropes the animal's horns."

Her son and the internet were best friends. Ryan must have researched team roping before they'd hit the road this morning.

"The Cash brothers need to beat the ten-second mark to take over first place," the announcer said.

The fans quieted and the rodeo helpers readied the chute. Marsha's eyes remained on Will. At thirty-two he might be one of the older cowboys in rodeo, but he looked sexier today than he had in high school. His crimson shirt hugged his muscular chest and the silver championship belt buckle showed off his lean hips. When other guys in their high-school class were losing their hair and sporting beer bellies, Will was all lean, hard muscle.

"They've got the barrier in place across the header's box." The announcer chuckled. "Don't blink or you'll miss all the action."

Marsha held her breath when the gate opened and the steer broke through the flag barrier and ran for freedom. Porter swung his rope twice before it sailed through the air and over the steer's head. Porter turned the animal and Will roped the its hind legs on the first try.

"Well, folks, after adding in the penalty, it looks like the Cash brothers clocked in at thirteen seconds. Better luck next time, cowboys."

"They're not very good." Ryan slouched in his seat.

Marsha felt the urge to defend Will—it wasn't his fault that she'd put him in a position of having to impress a son he hadn't known existed until a few days ago—but she held her tongue. Ryan rarely spoke harshly about others. Did he expect his father to find fault with him? Wanting to ease his anxiety she offered him an out. "We can drive home and meet your father later."

"No." He sat up straight. "Let's find him." Translation—let's get this over with.

As they navigated the crowds, Marsha looked for a red shirt in the sea of Marlboro men. Ryan inched closer to her side and she wished she possessed a magic wand that could cast a spell on father and son, ensuring their first meeting was the stuff of fairy tales and happily-ever-afters.

"There he is." The Cash brothers were conversing with a rodeo helper. Will glanced her way and she pasted a smile on her face as she and Ryan approached. If her gaze hadn't drifted down his body she would have missed the way he tensed when he noticed Ryan.

Will's brown eyes softened and Marsha's knees went

weak with relief. Father and son hadn't exchanged a word but the warmth in Will's gaze gave her hope that the meeting would go smoothly.

Will held out his hand. "Nice to meet you, Ryan."

"Yes, sir." Ryan barely squeezed Will's hand before shoving his fingers inside the pocket of his khaki shorts.

"This is your uncle, Porter," Will said.

Porter shook Ryan's hand. "What do you think of the rodeo so far?"

Ryan shrugged.

"How would you like a tour of the cowboy ready area, Ryan?" Will asked.

"While you and your dad do that, I'll buy your mom a hot dog." The innocent expression on Porter's face didn't fool Marsha. He was helping his older brother finagle time alone with his son.

"How does that sound, Ryan?" Marsha asked.

Another shrug.

"When and where shall we meet up?" she asked.

"How about right here in an hour?" Porter said. "Will and I have a second go-round this afternoon."

"Sounds good." Marsha turned away, but Will snagged her arm. She shivered at the feel of his calloused fingers against her skin and an image of the two of them tangled up in the backseat of his pickup flashed before her eyes. Good Lord, she was in big trouble if it only took a simple touch from Will to send her heart slamming into her rib cage. She waited for him to speak. Instead, he released her and said nothing.

Marsha walked off with Porter but after a few yards glanced over her shoulder. Ryan's gaze was glued to his shoes while Will spoke.

"They'll be fine," Porter said as if he sensed Marsha's urge to rescue her son.

She had no one to blame but herself for putting Ryan in this awkward position and she deserved to suffer right along with him.

"YOU EVER BEEN to a rodeo before?" Will asked, aware that Ryan had yet to make eye contact with him. Didn't the kid realize he was nervous, too?

"When I was little, Grandpa and Grandma took me to one."

Will stared at the top of his son's head as a swell of emotion—guilt, anxiety, curiosity, wariness and hope—threatened to drown him. He broke out in a sweat at the memory of meeting his own father for the first time. The circumstances had been different—his father had known all along about Will and he hadn't cared. In this case, Will hadn't known Ryan existed, but that important detail probably didn't matter to the teen.

God, he resented Marsha for putting him in this tight spot.

*Yeah, right. That's not what you felt a few moments ago when you touched her.*

Ignoring the voice in his head he focused on Ryan, wishing he had a manual on fatherhood—a guide to tell him how to handle this meeting.

A burning sensation attacked Will's eyes as he realized this might possibly be the most humbling moment of his existence—walking alongside the young man whose life he'd wanted ended before it had begun.

*Too late for a do-over.* The only path remaining for him and Ryan to travel was the one right in front of them. "C'mon, I'll show you what goes on behind the chutes." He changed directions, but Ryan didn't follow, his gaze avoiding Will's. Obviously the teen was uncomfortable in his presence.

"If you want, you can text your mom and tell her that you're ready to leave." Ryan's head snapped up and father and son looked each other in the eye. The teen was only a couple of inches shorter than Will. He and his son might not have the same eye color but they shared the same dark eyebrows, hair color and strong jaw.

"I don't like rodeos," Ryan said.

The confession stung Will, but he tried not to take it personally. It wasn't Ryan's fault that he'd been raised by a single mother and probably hadn't been exposed to a lot of *guy* activities growing up. "What do you like to do?" Will motioned for Ryan to move aside when a cowgirl walked a horse past them.

"I read a lot."

Will didn't read much because he got headaches from the letters in the words jumping in front of his eyes. In third grade, he'd been diagnosed with dyslexia and had read only enough to get by in his classes and graduate high school. College had never been on his radar. He motioned to a pair of chairs outside the restroom area. After they sat down, he asked, "What kinds of books do you read?"

Ryan's expression lightened. "My favorite book is *The Hobbit*."

Will had heard about the movie but hadn't seen it. "Who's your favorite character?"

"Bilbo Baggins. Do you like Tolkien's writing?"

"Sure," he lied.

"I read *The Lord of the Rings*."

At least Will had seen that movie.

"Tolkien was a professor at Pembroke College in Oxford, England. I want to go to college there, too."

The arena walls closed in on Will and he changed the subject. "Have you ever ridden a horse?"

"No."

"Would you like to? Your uncle Mack works at a dude ranch and he can take us on a trail ride."

"What's a trail ride?"

"Natural paths in the desert that horses can easily navigate."

Ryan shook his head. "No, thanks."

"Do you like fishing? We've got a water hole on the farm that—"

"I don't like fishing."

"Have you ever fished before?"

"No, but I don't think I'd like it."

Will dragged a hand down his face. Finding a common interest with his son was proving difficult. "Do you have any big plans for this summer?"

"Not really. I got a Kindle for my birthday and downloaded a lot of books before we drove out here."

Will didn't even know when his son had been born. "When was your birthday?"

"February twelfth."

"Three days before my birthday." Ryan didn't comment. "Besides reading, what other hobbies do you have?"

"I like to play chess with my grandpa."

*Swell.* Will played checkers but not chess.

"What grade in school are you?"

"This fall I'll be a freshman at the high school where Mom teaches."

Once Marsha had gone off to college in California,

Will had lost track of her—not that he'd tried to keep tabs on her whereabouts. He'd assumed she'd had an abortion so he'd moved on. If he'd asked around about her the first year she'd moved away, maybe he'd have learned she'd had a baby.

*But you didn't ask about her.*

He could have spoken with Marsha's parents or talked to her best friend Hillary Bancroft, who worked at the hair salon in town, but Will hadn't—because he hadn't wanted to know if Marsha had kept their baby. His worst nightmare would have been becoming a father and his eighteen-year-old mind insisted he was better off remaining in the dark.

"What subject does your mother teach?" He and Marsha hadn't spoken more than ten sentences to each other the night of the prom, but he did remember her saying she'd wanted to earn a teaching degree.

"Chemistry."

"That's a tough subject."

"Not really. I plan to take AP chemistry and physics before I graduate from high school."

Will had no idea what AP meant, but he assumed that his son had inherited his mother's IQ. If there was any blessing in this whole mess, it was that Will hadn't passed on the gene for dyslexia to his son. "What are your plans after you graduate high school?"

"I'm going to apply to Stanford, Harvard and Yale."

"Those are top-rated colleges. That's pretty ambitious."

"And don't forget Oxford University. Mom says I have to go to the school that offers me the most financial aid and scholarships."

Will's heart raced. Now that he knew he had a son,

he'd have to pay child support, which he intended to do, but how could he pay a hefty tuition bill on a small-town construction worker's salary? "Do you know what you want to study?"

"Probably physics."

"Great." The more Will learned about Ryan the dumber he felt and the less confident he was that he and his son would ever become close.

Ryan fidgeted in his chair and Will sensed the kid was eager to end their discussion. "You hungry?" he asked.

"Sure."

"Let's grab a hot dog and find your mom." This afternoon couldn't end soon enough. Will hadn't felt this insignificant since the day he'd confronted his biological father.

Fast forward twenty-two years and nothing had changed—he was still irrelevant.

"I'M DISAPPOINTED IN you, daughter."

Marsha had walked in the door less than a minute ago after a stressful afternoon at the rodeo and now her father was ready to face off with her.

"Let's take a walk." He gave her no choice but to tag along.

Feet dragging, she strolled with him across the patio and alongside the house to the front yard. Not until she and Ryan were driving home from the rodeo had she realized the extent of her exhaustion. She hadn't had a decent night's sleep since she'd made the decision to tell Will about Ryan. She wished she'd had a chance to talk with Will in private before they'd left the rodeo, but he and Porter had to prepare for their event and Ryan hadn't wanted to stay and watch.

When they reached the end of the sidewalk, her father continued along the path that led to the church—his silence made Marsha nervous. She'd asked her mother to break the news about Will while she and Ryan were at the rodeo, hoping her father would work through his anger before she returned. The stern look on his face convinced her that her plan had backfired.

Marsha had been a good daughter through the years but having a child out of wedlock had hurt and embarrassed the pastor in front of his parishioners and members of the community. Nonetheless, he was a loving man and had forgiven her and embraced his grandson— for that she'd always be grateful.

"I'm sorry, Dad." The words sounded inadequate, but what else could she say?

"Why did you keep us in the dark about William Cash?"

This was tricky. Her father would bend over backward to help a person in need and his actions always demonstrated his faith. However, years ago she'd learned that the man she'd believed walked on water was human and possessed prejudices like everyone else. "I didn't tell you, because I knew you disliked the Cash family."

He stopped walking. "I've never said—"

"You called them heathens the night I told you I was going to the prom with Will." Marsha had gotten a glimpse of her father's humanness that evening. He'd spouted a fiery speech, insisting she was too good for the likes of a Cash boy. She'd never heard him talk that way before but that night he hadn't been a pastor—he'd been a father, trying to protect his only child and he'd let nothing stand in his way. Not even God.

They cut across the parking lot to the reflection garden behind the church and sat in the shade on a stone bench.

"Did he refuse to marry you?" her father asked.

"I hardly knew Will." But she would have married him in a heartbeat if he'd proposed to her.

"You told him about the baby?"

She wouldn't lie to her father to protect Will. "Yes, I told him."

"Doesn't surprise me that he wanted nothing to do with Ryan." He scuffed the toe of his shoe against the gravel. "Has Ryan been asking questions about his father?"

"No."

"That's odd. You asked all kinds of questions about your parents before you were in kindergarten."

She'd asked questions because her parents had been open with her about her adoption. "I told Ryan years ago that if he was curious about his father, I'd be more than happy to talk about him."

"Why do you think he hasn't asked about William?"

"Because you're like a father to him. You've always been there for Ryan. Given him advice, guidance and love. Honestly, I don't believe Ryan feels as if he's missing out on anything by not having a father."

"I won't always be here for my grandson."

She squeezed his hand. They hadn't talked about his cancer since she'd arrived for the summer and she wasn't ready to now. "Give Will a chance, Dad. Please."

"I'll think about it." He retreated to the far side of the

garden where he bowed his head in front of the statue of Mary. Marsha left him in peace as the doubts in her head went to war with the hope in her heart.

## Chapter Four

"What happened?"

Will stopped on his way to the bunkhouse when Conway crossed his path.

"Porter and I came in fourth."

"That's not what I meant," Conway said.

"I'm not in the mood to talk." Will continued walking and his brother fell into step beside him.

"Things didn't go well?"

Will didn't have a chance to answer before the farmhouse door opened and his nephews raced outside.

"Uncle Will! Uncle Will!"

*Oh, hell.* He could easily ignore his brother but not the twins. He waited for the boys and Bandit to catch up. When the trio skidded to a stop, the dog slammed into the boys' legs, almost knocking them to the ground.

"Did you and Uncle Porter win a buckle?" Miguel asked.

"No, but we came close."

"Dad, can we go with Uncle Will to his next rodeo?" Javier spoke.

"If your uncle says it's okay."

A sliver of jealousy worked its way beneath Will's skin when he considered how fortunate Conway was that the twins idolized him. At least his nephews believed their uncle Will led an exciting life, because he went to rodeos and built things—unlike his son who'd rather stick his head in a book and read all day than watch his father rope a steer.

Will silently cursed himself for the uncharitable thought. A thirty-minute talk with Ryan had hardly made a dent in getting to know the young man. He ruffled the boys' hair and pointed to the dog. "Looks like Bandit wants to play catch."

The Lab understood the word *catch* and raced across the lawn, snatching the tennis ball from the ground in front of the porch. As soon as the boys ran after their four-legged pal, Conway spoke. "What happened with Ryan today?"

"I don't want to talk about it." Will went inside the bunkhouse where he hung his cowboy hat on the hook above his bed, then sat on the mattress and stared into space.

"You want me to call Johnny?" Conway hovered in the doorway.

Will was only a year younger than the eldest Cash brother but his siblings had elected Johnny head of the family after Grandpa Ely had died. "Johnny can't fix this." If his brother could, he wouldn't have hesitated seeking his advice. The problem was that no matter what Will did or said, he'd fall short in Ryan's eyes.

"When do the rest of us get to meet Ryan?" Conway asked.

"I don't know." He glared until his brother got the message and closed the door on his way out.

Will didn't give a crap that he'd been rude. He felt like a bear with a thorn in his paw and he wasn't fit for company. He stared at the ceiling. What was he supposed to do next? Was the ball in his court? Ryan's? Or was Marsha calling the shots?

*Marsha.*

Man, had she changed—and all in good ways. This afternoon she'd worn a pair of slim-fitting jeans and boots. The pink western shirt with black trim accentuated her breasts and had drawn the eye of more than a few cowboys. She hardly looked old enough to be the mother of a teenager.

An image of her walking down the hall in high school, head bent over the stack of books in her arms, popped into his mind. Today, she'd stood before him confident she could handle any obstacle in her way. He sure in heck could have used some of her self-assurance when he'd been introduced to his son.

*Why Marsha?* Why had he gotten the daughter of a church pastor pregnant? Their date to the prom had only happened because Buck had suggested he take Marsha after Will's first choice, Linda Snyder—the cheerleader he'd had a crush on—turned him down flat, claiming she'd have to be desperate before she'd be seen with a Cash boy. Will had taken Marsha to show Linda that if a Cash boy was good enough for a pastor's daughter…

The joke had been on him. In the end, the pastor's daughter hadn't believed Will good enough, otherwise she'd have told him she'd kept his baby instead of waiting until circumstances beyond her control had forced her to tell the truth.

The bunkhouse door opened and Will braced himself for an interrogation. "I told you to get lost, Conway."

"I'm not Conway."

*Buck.* This day couldn't get much worse.

"I ran into Porter at the drive-in. He said you guys took fourth place."

Will swung his legs off the side of the bed and sat up. There was no peace, living with three brothers. If he needed space to think, he was better off taking a drive or a walk in the desert.

"How'd your meeting with Ryan go?"

"I assumed you'd have heard by now." Will stood and faced his brother.

"Why would you think that? I've been fixing cars at Troy's garage all day."

The frustration and anger Will had kept bottled up inside him threatened to explode if he didn't have it out with Buck right now. "You knew for over a year that Ryan was my son and you didn't tell me."

"I made a promise to Marsha—"

"Forget Marsha! I'm your flesh and blood. You were supposed to have my back and you betrayed me. I don't know how your conscience allowed you to sleep at night."

Buck's eyes widened.

"It should have never come to this."

"What do you mean?" Buck watched him warily.

"You knew she'd had a baby years ago and although you didn't see Ryan when you stopped by her place… couldn't you put two and two together and solve the fatherhood puzzle?"

"I asked her who Ryan's father was but she wouldn't tell me."

"And then there's the big question…why you never mentioned to me or any of our brothers that Marsha had had a baby." Will moved closer, getting right up in Buck's grill. "None of us knew you'd seen her in California."

"I don't know why you'd expect me to mention Marsha. You only went to the prom with her to get even with Linda what's-her-name." Buck pointed a finger. "You didn't care about Marsha."

"It doesn't matter whether I cared or not. We made a baby!"

Buck clenched his hands but remained silent.

"Because of you my son has grown into a teenager I have nothing in common with. Zero. Zilch."

"Give it a chance, Will. He'll—"

"Do you know he hates rodeo? And get this…Ryan loves to read and I can't read worth a damn." Will needed someone to blame for the situation he was in and Buck was an easy target because he'd been closest to Marsha. "Ryan's never going to look up to me as a father."

Buck's face paled.

"You're my brother! You should have been looking out for me. Once you learned I was Ryan's father you should have told me."

Buck's brooding expression pissed Will off and he punched him in the face, splitting his lip. Buck stumbled sideways but didn't raise a fist.

"You're right. I should have told you."

"Coward!" Will punched Buck in the chest. "You robbed me and my son of fourteen years together!" Will took an apple from the fruit bowl on the table and threw it. Buck dodged the missile, which hit the aluminum wall and made a dent.

"Would it have mattered if you knew you'd fathered Ryan?"

Will gaped.

"You always said you never wanted to be a father."

Will cringed at Buck's statement. His brother had

hit a nerve and Will tried to defend himself. "What eighteen-year-old is ready to become a father? I didn't have a steady job. I'd barely managed to graduate from high school." And their mother had died earlier that year. The family had been in turmoil and he'd been in no shape to raise a child. "Go away."

"Let me make it up to you." Buck's pleading tone grated on Will's nerves. "I'll talk to Marsha and—"

"No." Will sliced the air with his hand. "You've done enough damage."

"Then tell me how to make it right."

"Leave."

"What?"

"Get out of town," Will said.

"For how long?" The whispered question hung in the air.

"Until I figure things out with Marsha and Ryan." Will didn't need his brother interfering when he was searching for a way to fit into his son's life. If Buck hung around, Marsha might run to him when she had a disagreement with Will over Ryan.

Buck opened his mouth but no words came out. It must have been a trick of the light that made his brother's eyes look watery.

The crushing pain in Will's chest pushed the air from his lungs. Damn it, he wasn't the bad guy. Buck had betrayed him.

So why did he feel as if he'd just kicked his brother in the balls?

"WHAT ARE YOU DOING HERE?" Will asked when he spotted Johnny walking along the path to the fishing hole.

Shell-shocked after meeting his son yesterday and

then brawling with Buck, Will had taken his pole and escaped to the one place he could find peace and quiet on the farm. Or so he'd thought.

"I wanted to find out how things went with Ryan," Johnny said.

"I don't want to talk about Ryan."

"Okay. Let's talk about Buck. I heard you told him to take off."

"What if I did?"

"Troy's pretty pissed at you."

"Troy can find another mechanic to fix his cars." Will expected his brother to do an about-face, but Johnny stayed put—he was as stubborn as Will.

"You'd better learn how to deal with your situation, because I won't let you tear this family apart."

"No one's tearing anything apart. Besides, what does it matter if Buck's gone for a while? These days we all go our separate ways."

"You might not care, but Shannon's due date is two weeks away. I'd hoped to have my entire family here to welcome my son or daughter into the world."

*Well, shit.* Will had been caught up in his own situation and had forgotten about Shannon and the baby. "I'll talk to Buck and apologize."

"Good luck with that."

"What do you mean?"

"Buck's not answering his phone, and I bet he won't pick up when he sees your number."

Will set the pole on the ground, then paced in front of the pond. "What do you want me to do, Johnny?" The look of disappointment in his older brother's eyes cut him to the core.

"Buck told me the reason you sent him away."

"Hey, I'm not the one who was disloyal to a brother. Buck should have spoken up for me when I couldn't." Will winced. His shout had probably scattered the fish to the bottom of the pond.

"Buck isn't the one to blame, Will. Marsha hid your son from you."

Will searched for a rock and when he found a decent-size one he kicked it twenty yards. Johnny was right. Why was it easier to let Marsha's trespass slide and nail Buck's hide to the wall for his?

*Because Buck's kin. And it hurts a lot more when family betrays you.*

Will didn't want to care what Marsha thought of him, because he'd never measure up in her eyes or Pastor Bugler's, but what Ryan thought of him mattered. He wanted a chance to earn his son's respect.

Johnny nodded to the pond. "While you're fishing maybe you should consider your role in this situation."

"What are you talking about?"

"The afternoon we caught Dixie and Gavin taking a shower together before they got married."

"What about that day?"

"We all got into an argument in the hallway and Buck let it slip that Marsha had told him you'd gotten her pregnant."

"Yeah."

"You could have asked Buck when he and Marsha had talked."

"Why would I care when she told him?"

"You didn't care, Will, because you didn't want to ask Buck if Marsha had kept the baby."

"Marsha told me she was getting an abortion and I believed her."

*No, she told you not to worry about the baby, that she'd take care of it.*

Will rubbed a hand down his jaw. He'd wanted to believe she'd meant she'd abort the baby but fear that she might not had kept him from seeking the truth.

Johnny quirked an eyebrow. "You having unprotected sex with Marsha set in motion everyone's destiny— including yours." Johnny turned away.

"Wait. Tell me what to do. How do I make this right?"

The sympathetic expression on Johnny's face sent a sharp pain through Will's chest. "I don't have any answers. You'll have to find your own way through this, but don't forget…"

Will swallowed hard.

"What's done is done. All you can change now is the future."

When Johnny disappeared from view, Will sank to the ground and stared into space. His brother was right. The only option was to move forward and find a place for himself in his son's life. Will waited a half hour for a fish to bite, then packed up his gear. When he reached the barn, he noticed the pile of new lumber by the front porch.

*Damn.* He'd promised the twins he'd build Bandit a doghouse this weekend. An idea came to mind—he'd ask Ryan to help and hope that the twins' constant babble would put his son at ease.

"I'M SO EXCITED," Hillary Bancroft said when Marsha slipped into the stylist's chair at the Bee Luv Lee Hair Salon. "I can't believe you and Ryan are staying in Stagecoach for the whole summer."

"I'm looking forward to spending more time with

my father," Marsha said. *And Will*. She wanted to get to know her son's father and find out what kind of man he'd become.

Hillary draped a black cape over Marsha and fussed with her wavy locks. "How's your dad feeling?"

"Dad's slowed down since our last trip home." There was no need to go into the details of her father's battle with prostate cancer—Hillary and her twelve-year-old daughter were members of the Mission Community Church.

"What does Ryan think about being stuck in the desert for two and a half months?"

"That's what I wanted to talk to you about." Marsha glanced across the room where the new owner of the salon, Rosie Davis, was styling Fiona Wilson's gray hair. Fiona had been Marsha's English teacher in high school but had since retired. Marsha glanced in the mirror and caught Hillary watching her.

"Rosie's making a bank run as soon as she finishes Fiona's hair. We'll have the place to ourselves for a few minutes."

*Good*. Marsha didn't want Hillary learning Will was Ryan's father through the Stagecoach grapevine.

"Are we doing highlights today and trimming the ends?"

"Highlights," Marsha said.

"I'll mix up your color."

After Hillary disappeared, Rosie twirled Fiona's chair and Marsha smiled at the schoolteacher. "Any summer plans, Fiona?"

"Nothing too exciting," Fiona said. "Now how old is that son of yours?"

"Ryan turned fourteen this past February."

"It's not too early to discuss colleges."

"No worries there." Marsha laughed. "Ryan has his top four already picked out."

Fiona closed her eyes when Rosie reached for the can of hair spray.

"Ryan would love to study abroad in England, but that's not in the budget," Marsha said.

"Make sure he applies for scholarships," Fiona said.

"I will. I learned from the best."

Fiona beamed at the compliment. Without the English teacher's help in high school, Marsha wouldn't have landed a full-ride scholarship to the University of California in Los Angeles.

"Fiona, tell Marsha about your new boyfriend," Rosie grinned.

"It's nothing serious." Blushing, Fiona got out of her chair. "You probably don't know him. Clive Douglas. He owns the Triple D Ranch."

Of course Marsha knew the Douglas family. Her father had made trips to the ranch over the years, trying to convince the single father to bring his three children to church, which he'd done—but only on Christmas and Easter.

"That's exciting, Fiona," Marsha said. "I'm happy for you."

"Clive's daughter Shannon is expecting a baby in a couple of weeks."

"Really?" Why hadn't Marsha's mother mentioned the news?

"Shannon married Johnny Cash. You remember the Cash boys, don't you?" Fiona shook her head. "Those youngin's were nothing but trouble in school. I had them all in my literature class but the one who exasperated me the most was Willie Nelson. He never did his homework."

Marsha swallowed a giggle. What would Will think if he knew his former teacher referred to him as Willie Nelson?

"I never could understand why the boys' mother named them all after country-and-western singers. The rascals got into more fights over their names than all the other kids combined."

Marsha considered the Cash brothers' names unique but kept her opinion to herself. Of the six brothers, Willie and Merle were the only ones who chose to use a nickname.

"That Johnny Cash is a nice young man." Fiona pulled out her credit card and handed it to Rosie. "Johnny's brother Conway married a single mother of five-year-old twins this past spring. Won't be long before the rest of the brothers find wives and settle down."

Marsha sympathized with Will and his siblings. Because of their mother's numerous affairs, the Cash brothers had been the subject of gossip for years, and now Marsha was adding fire to the fuel by making it public that Will had fathered her son.

"Conway took over the family pecan farm and he's settled right into fatherhood." Fiona signed her credit slip. "That man loves those twins as if they were his own flesh and blood. After growing up without one, who'd have believed any of the Cash boys would make good fathers?"

"Rosie outdid herself on your curls today, Fiona," Hillary said when she returned with Marsha's hair tint.

"Thank you, dear." Fiona nodded to Rosie. "See you in two weeks."

Once the door closed behind Fiona, Rosie put on her sweater. "That darned bank is so cold." She removed the money bag from beneath the counter. "I'm stopping at the drive-in for lunch. Do either of you want to place an order?"

"No, thanks," Marsha and Hillary spoke simultaneously.

After Rosie disappeared, Hillary rolled her eyes. "She acts all nice to me in front of customers, but when we're alone, she's snippy."

"Why?"

"Because I cut hair better than she does and some of her clients are asking for me now." Hillary waved her magic comb. "Never mind Rosie. You were going to tell me how Ryan feels about spending the summer at your parents' house."

"Ryan doesn't know his grandfather's health has taken a turn for the worse. My parents didn't want me to tell him until we got here."

"That's going to be a tough conversation," Hillary said.

"That isn't the only thing he's going to be dealing with." Marsha's gaze avoided Hillary's in the mirror. "I introduced Ryan to his father yesterday."

Hillary gasped. "Ryan's father lives in Stagecoach?"

"Yes." Marsha had never told Hillary who'd fathered Ryan. Her friend had assumed it was a young man she'd met in California the summer after their high-school graduation.

"Wow. I would have never believed you'd slept with a local guy." Hillary said.

"It happened the night of the prom."

Hillary gasped. "You slept with Will Cash?"

Marsha nodded.

"Do your parents know?"

"Yes."

Hillary continued applying the color and folding the sheets of foil over the strands of hair until Marsha looked like a science experiment. "I bet the pastor wasn't pleased with the news."

"He's taking it better than I expected. And it turns out my mother guessed a few years ago, because she picked up on the resemblance between Ryan and Will."

"I've only seen Will from a distance over the years. I'm not sure I could tell."

"The older Ryan gets the more he looks like Will."

"What does Ryan think of his father?"

"The jury is still out." Marsha hoped father and son would grow closer.

"I don't see them having much in common."

Hillary had voiced what Marsha had been thinking herself.

"When's Will going to see Ryan next?"

"Probably today. Ben Wallace's construction company is building the new wing on the church."

Hillary whistled. "You mean Will's going to work right under your father's nose all summer?"

"Looks that way."

"Oh, honey. You and I are going to have to schedule a weekly happy-hour date."

Marsha laughed. "I was hoping you'd volunteer to be my therapist."

"For the price of a margarita you can cry on my shoulder as long as you want." Hillary pointed toward the window. "Rosie's here."

Too bad—Marsha had been working up the courage

to ask Hillary if she'd heard any gossip about Will's love life.

Marsha closed her eyes, half listening to Hillary and Rosie gossip. Her mind drifted to Will. He was better-looking today than he'd been in high school. He might only be a few inches taller than Marsha but what he lacked in height he more than made up for in a rock-hard body. And he wore his once shaggy hair neatly trimmed, which lent him an air of respectability and maturity—she could almost envision him wearing a tux and escorting her to a faculty party.

Never mind her father being exposed to Will all summer. What about her? When she made eye contact with Will, all she could think about was kissing him.

## Chapter Five

"He looks like you."

"Yeah, he does." Will climbed a step on the ladder and used a staple gun to attach plastic sheeting to the rear wall of the church. His boss, Ben, stood on a second ladder twenty feet away, securing his end of the covering. Once they protected the sanctuary from dirt and construction dust, they'd tear down a portion of the wall to make room for a hallway that would lead to the new classroom wing.

"I can't believe you didn't know you had a son."

Will didn't make a habit of sharing his private business with others, but he'd rather his boss heard the news from him than an embellished tale from an inebriated cowboy in a bar.

"So you lost touch with Marsha over the years?" Ben asked.

Lost touch? After Marsha had told Will she was pregnant and he'd insisted she have an abortion, he'd gone out of his way to avoid her and the pastor. "She moved to California the summer we graduated and I never saw her again." Will popped in the final staple and descended the ladder.

"Man, I'd be pissed if I'd gotten a girl pregnant and she hadn't told me."

Will's chest tightened with guilt, but he took the coward's way out and said, "Everybody has their reasons for making the choices they do." He could picture how nervous Marsha had been, facing her parents alone. He never would have guessed the girl he'd known in high school would possess the determination and courage needed to raise a child on her own. To put it bluntly, Will was in awe of the woman.

*And she's way out of your league.*

He knew that. Just because they had a son together and Marsha wanted him to grow closer to Ryan didn't mean *she* wanted to get close to him, too. "I'll fetch the weights from your pickup bed and set them across the bottom of the sheet to help hold it in place."

Will couldn't escape the church fast enough. He didn't want to discuss Ryan—not when he still grappled with the fact that he was a father. He hadn't slept well last night—his rest plagued with nightmares of the day he'd traveled to Tucson to confront his own father.

Until he'd learned about Ryan, Will hadn't acknowledged how deeply his father's abandonment had scarred him. His first thought had been to do the exact opposite of what his father had done to him—instead of ignoring Ryan, he'd go out of his way to be with him. Then he'd recalled Ryan's lukewarm reception at the rodeo and had doubted himself, assuming his son needed more space.

Halfway across the parking lot Will saw Marsha walking along the path to the church. She waved and he raised his hand, the gesture awkward—everything about their situation felt uncomfortable.

Glad he wore his mirrored sunglasses, he watched her curvy hips swish-sway as she approached. She wore khaki shorts and a white T-shirt with an image of a green dragon on the front. Cedar High was printed above the image—must be the school where she taught. The shirt was a men's cut, but it didn't conceal her feminine curves and Will silently cursed his dry mouth. If his stomach wasn't tied in knots, he might chuckle at how the tables had been turned on him. He'd been the guy Marsha had had a crush on—according to Buck. Now he was the one drooling over her.

"Good morning." She stopped a few feet away—not far enough to prevent the scent of her perfume from reaching his nose.

"'Morning."

"Mom's making fresh lemonade. Would you and Ben like a glass?"

He'd brought his own jug of water, but he said, "Sure."

She wrung her hands, the action reminding him of the day she'd stopped at his locker and had asked what color tie he'd planned to wear to the prom. Had he worn a suit and tie that night?

She glanced at the church then at her parents' house—lemonade wasn't the only thing on her mind. "I was hoping Ryan could help you today."

So much for easing into fatherhood. "Help how?"

"Maybe he could hand you tools or..." She tilted her chin, the motion freeing the hair she'd tucked behind her ear. The silky strands brushed her cheek and he stuffed his fingers into his pants pocket to keep from touching her curls to find out if they were as soft as they looked.

"Is Ryan bored?" Will sympathized with the teenager—

the kid was used to city life and probably went stir-crazy stuck at his grandfather's house.

"He's not bored, he's—"

"Hey, Will, what's taking—" Ben nodded. "Hi, Marsha."

"Hello, Ben." Her smile drew Will's gaze to her mouth. She wasn't a woman who wore a lot of makeup, but the pink tint covering her lips reminded him of their heated kisses prom night. He'd been her first French kiss, but he assumed she'd had numerous kisses since him—a woman as pretty and sexy as Marsha probably had men fawning over her.

"How's the pastor feeling?" Ben asked.

"Dad's excited about the new classroom wing. He'll be out later to check on your progress."

"Look forward to seeing him." Ben cleared his throat. "I'll take in the weights." He lifted the heavy discs out of the truck bed, then excused himself.

"If Ryan's not bored, why do you want him to help?" Will asked.

Her blue eyes darkened before she looked down and drew circles in the dirt with the toe of her sneaker. "I don't know what to do."

Will had lost track of the conversation. "Do about what?"

"Ryan's obsession with reading."

What did reading have to do with Ryan helping Will today? He caught Ben poking his head outside to check on them. "Marsha, I can't talk right now."

She jerked as if he'd slapped her. "Never mind." She spun, but he stepped into her path and blocked her escape.

"I can talk after work," he said.

She jutted her chin. "That's okay. I'll figure it out on my own."

Will stared at her retreating figure, a slow burn spreading through his chest. Whatever issue Marsha was having with Ryan wasn't Will's fault. And how could she expect him to fix the problem when he hardly knew his son?

"Everything okay?" Ben asked when Will entered the church.

"Yeah." Will checked the plastic sheeting, making sure there were no gaps. Then he put on his safety goggles and grabbed a sledgehammer.

The first whack jarred his shoulder and sent plaster chips spewing in all directions. He raised the hammer again, but Ben's cell phone rang. When Ben ended the call, Will asked, "What's going on?"

"That was the Yuma county clerk. She said I'm missing a building permit. I've got to drive into town and take care of this."

"Are we stopping for the day?"

"Hell, no." Ben glanced at the chapel ceiling. "I mean heck, no."

"While you're gone, I'll tear down this section of the wall to the studs," Will said. He waited until he heard Ben's truck pull away, then swung the hammer hard, splintering off a large chunk of stucco. Swing after swing, he demolished the wall, sweat pouring down his face and soaking his shirt. When he finished, he surveyed his work.

"You taking a break?"

Will jumped inside his skin. "Hey, Ryan."

"My mom said you wanted lemonade." He held out a plastic cup.

"Thanks. I could use some sugar after knocking out that wall." He swallowed a big gulp.

"Grandma doesn't put sugar in her lemonade."

Startled by the sourness Will sucked his cheeks in.

"Why is that wire in the wall?" Ryan examined the exposed mesh.

"The wire gives the stucco something to adhere to when it's applied."

"Oh." Ryan glanced behind him as if searching for a quick getaway.

Will hadn't forgotten that Marsha had asked if Ryan could help today. "How would you like to tear the wire out?"

"No, thanks." Ryan scuffed his shoe on the ground— a nervous habit he must have picked up from his mother.

"You sure? I've got an extra pair of work gloves and I could use the help."

"Okay." He didn't sound very enthusiastic.

Will tossed a pair of leather gloves at Ryan then motioned to the wall. "Take the corner and pull from the top down." Once Ryan gripped his section, Will said, "Pull."

Will yanked hard and his piece separated from the wood studs. Ryan continued tugging but the mesh remained intact. "I can't do it."

"Let me take a look." Will threaded his gloved fingers through the holes in the wire and pulled it free on the first try. "Nothing to it."

Ryan backed away. "I'm going inside."

"You don't want to help with the other sections?"

"I'd rather read."

Before the boy reached the door, Will said, "What are you doing this Saturday?"

"Nothing."

"I promised my nephews I'd build a house for their dog. Would you like to come out to the farm and help us?"

"Maybe."

"Think about it then let me know later this week."

"What kind of dog?" Ryan asked.

"A black Lab named Bandit."

"How old are your nephews?"

"Five and they're twins."

"Okay. I'll help."

Talk about a quick turnaround.

"Can my mom come, too?"

The last thing Will needed was Marsha watching his every move with Ryan, but obviously his son didn't want to be alone with him. "Sure. Your mom's welcome to hang out at the farm."

Ryan nodded then left.

After tugging off the wire mesh Will spent the next hour cleaning up the mess and hauling the debris to the Dumpster in the parking lot. When he moved aside the protective sheet to make sure no debris had fallen inside the sanctuary, he came face-to-face with Pastor Bugler.

It had been years since Will had seen Marsha's father and the pastor's frailness shocked him—even his clothes hung loose on his frame. Hearing that someone had cancer was a whole lot different than seeing firsthand the effects of the disease on the person. He felt bad for Marsha and Ryan and predicted it would be an emotional summer for both of them.

"William."

Willie was the name printed on his birth certificate, but he didn't bother to correct the man. "Pastor Bugler."

"Under the circumstances I believe you should call me Jim."

Will had convinced himself that he was prepared for this moment, but he caught himself staring at the exit.

"I thought we should talk." The pastor patted the space beside him on the pew.

Will hadn't sat in a church pew since Johnny and Shannon had married—and that ceremony had lasted fifteen minutes.

"I don't know who I'm angrier with—you for taking advantage of my daughter or my daughter for letting you take advantage of her."

Will sensed what the pastor was thinking... *Any other man would have made a better father for my grandson than a Cash boy.*

"I'm not surprised you didn't offer to marry Marsha," he said. "But I am surprised that you didn't want to raise your child."

Marsha hadn't told the whole truth to her father. If Will was any kind of man at all, he needed to own up to his actions even though his honesty wouldn't earn him points with the pastor. He shoved a dirty hand through his sweat-dampened hair. "I told your daughter to get an abortion."

The disappointment in the pastor's eyes cut Will to the core.

"Don't look at me that way." He sprang from the pew and paced across the sanctuary. "You know I'm not cut out to be a father." His outburst echoed through the church.

"So you abandoned Ryan and forced my daughter to raise him on her own?"

"That's what my father did to me. I didn't know any other way."

"You're a liar, William Cash. You did know another way. Your grandfather never walked out on your grandmother, and he helped raise all of you hooligans." Marsha's father turned away, his spine bowed as if the truth was too heavy to carry.

"Hey!" Will shouted. "Your daughter said she'd take care of things, so I assumed she had. If I'd known she'd kept the baby…" *I would have helped raise my son.* Will couldn't make himself finish the lie. Not that it mattered—the pastor had left the church.

Before he demolished a second wall—with his fists—Will headed outside, stopping when he almost kicked over the glass of lemonade Ryan had delivered to him. He picked up the cup and stared at the tepid liquid. No matter what he did or how hard he tried, he'd come up short—if not in his son's eyes then in Marsha's and Pastor Bugler's.

Would he ever be able to banish the image of his birth father shutting the door in his face? It was mighty tempting to take the easy way out, but he'd already turned his back on Ryan once. He wouldn't do it again. In the end, if his son wanted nothing to do with him— so be it.

"What do you think of your dad?" Marsha's father asked Ryan Friday evening as they sat at the kitchen table studying a chessboard. Marsha eavesdropped from behind the laundry-room door.

"He's okay," Ryan said.

Her father ran with the lukewarm response. "Your

mom said you helped him in the church earlier this week."

"He asked me to pull off this wire stuff in the walls." A chair scraped against the tile floor, then the refrigerator door opened and she heard the pop of a soda-can tab.

"How'd it go?" her father asked.

"Not too good."

"What happened?"

"I tried to tug the mesh free, but it was hard and he had to help me. I'm not good at construction stuff."

Almost a week had passed since Ryan had met Will and he'd yet to ask Marsha any questions about him.

"I don't care for physical labor," her father said. "I'd rather save my energy for more important things."

If her father didn't keep his opinions about Will to himself she'd have to intervene.

"I'd rather read and study," Ryan said.

"You're like your mother. She values a good education and look how smart she is."

"Mom said she doesn't know if my dad went to college."

"I don't believe he did."

"Do you think he knows how to play chess?" Ryan asked.

"Probably not. But I'll always be your chess partner."

Marsha's eyes watered when she heard the hitch in her father's voice. He knew there would come a day when he'd no longer play chess with Ryan—a day she didn't want to think about.

"Do you like my dad, Grandpa?" A heavy silence filled the kitchen, then Ryan said, "You don't like him, do you?"

"Can't a man think about his next move?"

Her father was stalling. *C'mon, Dad, give Will a chance.*

"Check."

"Grandpa!"

Her father cleared his throat. "Ryan, I'm not sure how to answer your question about your father, because I don't really know him. His family didn't attend my church."

"Oh." More silence then Ryan said, "He wants me to help him and his nephews build a doghouse."

"When?"

"Tomorrow. He said Mom could come, if she wanted to."

This was the first Marsha had heard of Will inviting them to the farm. Her son shared everything with her—the good and the bad. That he hadn't mentioned building a doghouse suggested that he remained undecided about going.

"Do you want to help your dad?"

"Not really." There was a pause, then she heard Ryan say, "But I wouldn't mind seeing the dog. It's a Lab named Bandit."

Her son loved dogs, but she'd never allowed him to have one because she hadn't thought it fair to leave an animal home alone all day while she and Ryan were at school.

"If you don't want to go, you don't have to." Her father pushed his chair away from the table. "I'd planned to drive into Yuma tomorrow. I can drop you off at the library if you want."

Her father was trying to persuade Ryan not to spend time with Will. Marsha understood and sympathized with his fear of losing his grandson to Will, but he should know that Ryan's love for him was strong and true.

She lifted the wash-machine lid and closed it loudly, then stepped into the kitchen. "How's the game going?" she asked.

Her father frowned.

"Grandpa's beating me as usual."

"Grandpa's a tough opponent."

"Ryan said William asked—"

"Dad, his name is Will, not William." Everyone knew that the Cash brothers' mother, Aimee, had printed her sons' monikers on their birth certificates exactly the way their country-western namesakes spelled them, which proved a problem for Will because Willie was not a name most adult men prefer to be called.

"Will asked Ryan to help him build a doghouse," her father said.

Marsha pretended she hadn't overheard their conversation. "When?"

"Tomorrow," Ryan said. "You're invited, too."

"Sounds like fun," she said.

"Are you going to come with me?" Ryan asked.

"I don't know how much help I'll be, but I can pound a nail or two," Marsha said.

"We'll finish this game later," her father said. "I need to rest."

Marsha blocked Ryan when he tried to follow his grandfather out of the room. "How come you didn't tell me that Will invited you to the farm?"

He dropped his gaze and scuffed his shoe against the floor.

"Talk to me, Ryan. What's going through your mind?"

"I don't think he likes me."

"Will?"

Ryan nodded.

"What makes you say that?"

"When I couldn't pull out the wire, he said it was easy."

Now she understood why Ryan had remained holed up inside the house the rest of the week while Ben and Will worked.

"You should help build the doghouse," she said. "Besides, you love dogs."

"I guess we can go."

It hadn't taken much effort to sway Ryan, and Marsha hoped that meant he was considering giving Will a chance. "Set your alarm for eight-thirty. I want you to eat breakfast before we leave." Marsha poked him in the shoulder and teased, "I heard building a doghouse is strenuous work."

Ryan's mouth twitched as he struggled to contain a smile when he walked from the room. If she didn't know better, she'd believe he was looking forward to tomorrow.

Marsha, on the other hand, had mixed feelings about spending an entire day with Will. She worried that the crush she'd had on him all those years ago hadn't died. She'd counted on the physical attraction being there between them but not the vulnerability in Will's brown gaze that tugged at her heartstrings.

That she definitely hadn't counted on.

## Chapter Six

"Uncle Will?"

"What?" Will stopped sketching the plans for the doghouse and waited for Javier to speak.

"Is there gonna be room for Bandit's bed in there?"

"How big is his bed?"

The screen door banged against the side of the house and Miguel stepped onto the porch, carrying a massive dog pillow twice the size of him. Will rushed forward and took the pillow before the kid tripped and fell down the steps.

"You guys spoil Bandit." The twins must have talked their father into buying the Great Dane-size pillow. Conway was a softie when it came to the twins.

Will made a few tweaks to his sketch. "The pillow will be a tight fit, but I think it will work." He tried to envision himself as a father when Ryan had been the twins' age, but he couldn't. At twenty-four he'd been riding the rodeo circuit and working odd jobs to cover his entry fees. He wouldn't have made his son a priority.

The sound of a car engine met his ears and the boys raced across the yard, Bandit trailing behind them. Marsha's SUV came into view and as soon as she saw the kids, she slowed the car to a crawl.

Will's heart hammered inside his chest. He'd worked at the church all week and was used to seeing Marsha come and go but he hadn't spent an entire day with her. He was nervous—not because it was difficult to hide the fact that he found her attractive, but because he didn't feel like he was her equal. She'd gone to college and bettered herself while he remained behind and became a construction worker.

"Good morning," Marsha said after she got out of the car.

Will opened his mouth to speak but the words froze in his throat when the passenger-side door opened and Pastor Bugler stepped into view. "Pastor," Will said.

"William."

"'Morning, Ryan," Will said. The teen lifted a hand in greeting. Will motioned to the twins standing with him. "Javier and Miguel, this is my son, Ryan, his mother, Ms. Bugler, and his grandfather, Pastor Bugler."

"My dad says Uncle Will is the best builder in the whole world," Miguel said.

"Uncle Will's gonna build Bandit a doghouse." Javier walked up to Ryan and asked, "Are you gonna help us?"

Ryan nodded.

"This is Bandit." Miguel tugged on the dog's collar and dragged the animal over to Ryan. "My dad gave us Bandit for Christmas. You want to see his toys?"

"Sure." Ryan accompanied the boys and the dog inside the house.

Pastor Bugler chuckled. "Looks like you lost your workforce."

Will's brow broke out in a sweat as he faced off with Marsha and her father.

"How can we help?" Marsha asked.

"I forgot the nails. Wait here." As soon as Will entered the barn, he cursed out loud.

"What's wrong? Are the boys getting on your nerves?" Conway poked his head out from beneath the tractor engine. "I can ask Isi to keep them in the house if—"

"The twins are fine. Marsha's dad came along today."

"Why?"

*To spy on me.* "Heck if I know." Will had been nervous enough about spending the day with Ryan and Marsha without having the pastor's eyes watching his every move.

Conway got to his feet. "Don't let him ruin your day."

"How am I supposed to have a decent conversation with my son if the old man is eavesdropping?"

"I don't know, but you can't hide in here all day."

"You're right. See you later." Will took a box of nails from the shelf above the workbench. When he returned to the yard, he walked past Marsha and her father. "I'll holler inside the house for the boys." Halfway up the porch steps, he stopped. "Would you two like a bottled water?"

"No, thanks," Marsha said. Her father shook his head.

Will opened the screen door and shouted. "Hey, boys, we've got a doghouse to build."

The twins came outside with Bandit's toy basket and Ryan held the dog's favorite soccer ball. Bandit twirled in circles whining to play.

Ryan threw the soccer ball and the dog raced across the yard, then used his snout to push the ball. Ryan laughed and Will felt a warm sensation stir in his chest. Bandit's antics won over the pastor, too, because the old man grinned as he watched the activity. Maybe today wouldn't be as stressful as Will anticipated.

He called for the boys to stand in the shade of his grandmother's favorite tree—a twenty-five-foot desert willow. "The first thing we have to do," Will said, "is build a platform so the doghouse doesn't sit directly on the ground."

"How come Bandit's house can't sit on the ground?" Miguel asked.

Pastor Bugler put his hand on Miguel's shoulder. "If it rains, son, the floor of the doghouse would flood and Bandit would have to sleep on a soggy dog pillow."

Javier inched closer to the pastor. "Bandit likes water. We taught him to swim in the pond."

"Swimming is one thing, but I don't believe Bandit wants to sit in a muddy puddle," the pastor said.

"Bandit likes taking a bath." Miguel joined the conversation. "He shakes his bubbles all over us."

The pastor chuckled at the twins' chatter. While the boys entertained Marsha's father with Bandit stories, Will spoke to Ryan. "Have you ever used a nail gun before?"

Ryan shook his head.

He held up the nail gun and pointed out its features, then handed it to Ryan. "I'll hold these two boards together and you shoot the nail into the wood at a downward angle." Will aligned the ends of the boards but Ryan hesitated.

"Don't worry," he said. "If the nail doesn't go in the right way, we can remove it and do it again."

Ryan hesitated—what was the teen afraid of? When Will was his age, he'd been allowed to use his grandpa's hunting rifle and he'd put it to good use—shooting the occasional snake that nested under the front porch. Believing his son needed encouragement, he said, "It's like shooting a BB gun." When Ryan didn't respond, Will asked, "You've shot a BB gun before, haven't you?"

Ryan shook his head.

"Then we'll put BB-gun shooting on our list of things to do this summer." He nodded to the boards. "Give it a try." Ryan's hand shook when he pressed the nail gun against the wood. Will steadied his wrist. "You can't squeeze the trigger if your hand shakes. The nail might miss the wood and hit the boys or the dog." He winked. "And I don't think you want to shoot your mother with a nail."

Instead of finding humor in Will's words, Ryan set down the gun. "You do it. I don't want to."

"C'mon, Ryan, it's not a big deal." What was the kid so afraid of?

"Why don't I hold the wood together and you demonstrate how to use the tool?" Marsha said.

Will wasn't fooled by the calm tone in her voice. Her pretty blue eyes fired off warnings faster than the gun could shoot nails. What the heck had he done wrong now? "Sure." He handed the wood to Marsha, careful not to touch her—it was already difficult enough smelling her perfume and fresh-from-the-shower scent. In a matter of minutes the platform had been constructed. And during that short time the pastor had retreated to the porch where he sat on the swing with the twins and Ryan had gone off to play soccer with Bandit.

Marsha touched his arm. "I guess building a doghouse isn't all it's cracked up to be."

Her words barely registered with Will as a tingling sensation spread across his skin. His gaze shifted to her mouth and caught Marsha's tongue sliding over her lower lip. A sharp ache attacked his chest as he imagined kissing her…tasting the shiny gloss. Marsha's fingers slid off his arm, ending his fantasy.

"I put too much pressure on him, didn't I?" Will said.

She shook her head. "Being raised by a single mother has a few disadvantages. He hasn't been exposed to many traditional *guy* activities." Her gaze softened as she watched Ryan play with the dog.

Will might not have been there for the teen, but his son was fortunate to have a mother like Marsha—an idiot could tell how much she loved the kid.

"Haven't any of your boyfriends spent time with Ryan?"

"Boyfriends?" Marsha scoffed. "I'm too busy with my job and driving Ryan to and from all his school activities. If I have free time, I use it to catch up on sleep."

Marsha's confession shocked Will. With her looks and her body he'd have expected men to knock down her door to get a date with her. He had to know. "How many boyfriends have you had?"

"A couple." Her flirty smile faded. "I came close to saying yes to one man, but…"

Marsha had almost married? "What happened?"

She shook her head. "I don't know. He got along well with Ryan and Ryan liked him, but—"

"Hey, Will!" Conway's wife, Isi, stepped onto the porch and waved. "I put on a fresh pot of coffee. Why don't you let Ryan's mother come inside where it's cooler and we can visit."

*Saved by the bell.* Marsha had almost told Will *he'd* been the reason she hadn't married. After seeing Will again, she could no longer fool herself into believing she didn't have feelings for him.

"I'd love to sit inside for a spell." She walked off before Will had a chance to object. "I'm Marsha Bugler." She motioned to the swing. "This is my father, Pastor Bugler."

"Nice to meet you both. I'm Conway's wife, Isi." She smiled. "Pastor Bugler, I baked gingersnaps yesterday, would you like a few to go with your coffee?"

"I sure would, thank you."

"Will installed central air in the house a few months ago. You're welcome to sit inside," Isi said.

"No!" The twins pulled on the pastor's arms. "Stay here."

He chuckled. "I'll take my coffee and cookies on the porch."

"If you need a break from my boys feel free to join us in the kitchen." Isi held the door open for Marsha and they entered the house.

Marsha took a seat at the table. She'd never been inside Will's childhood home but from the looks of the kitchen there had been a lot of love inside the walls.

"Conway and I are in the process of remodeling the house—one room at a time. We're saving the kitchen for last."

"If you wait long enough the wallpaper might come back in style," Marsha said, admiring the miniature white-and-blue teapots against a rose-colored background.

Isi pointed to the black spot on the floor in front of the sink. "Can you imagine how many dishes their grandma Ada must have washed over the years to wear away the linoleum?"

"More than I would ever want to do."

"I hope your father doesn't mind the boys pestering him. Miguel and Javier can be a little overwhelming. Having a big family is new to them and they can't get enough of everyone's attention."

Marsha admired Isi's long black hair and pretty brown eyes. "Will mentioned that you and Conway married this past spring?"

Isi set a cup of coffee in front of Marsha, then poured a mug for herself. "That's right. And I have Will to thank for bringing us together." She carried a plate of cookies and a mug of coffee outside.

When Isi entered the kitchen again, Marsha asked, "Did Will fix you up on a date with Conway?"

"Heavens no. Conway and I had been friends for a couple of years." Isi smiled. "Unbeknownst to Conway he was falling in love with me, but he was running scared. He set me up with Will, thinking his brother was a safe bet."

"Was Will a safe bet?" Marsha cringed. She hadn't meant to speak the question out loud.

"No sparks. Will and I knew right away nothing was going to happen between us." Isi waved a hand in the air. "We tried a kiss to be sure."

Marsha ignored the burning sensation in her stomach. She assumed Will had kissed plenty of women since he took her to the prom, but she never expected to sit across the table and talk with one of them.

"It was obvious to me and Will that we were meant to be friends, but he made sure Conway believed he had romantic feelings for me."

"What did Conway do?"

Isi smiled. "He proposed."

At least Isi got her happily-ever-after. "Is Will dating anyone?"

"No, he hasn't had a girlfriend in a long while." She offered a hesitant smile. "If I can be nosey…what happened between you and Will? Conway said Will just learned Ryan was his son."

"It's a long story. I believed I was doing what was best for everyone by raising Ryan alone."

"But you changed your mind?"

Marsha nodded.

"Did Ryan ask about his father?"

As much as Marsha enjoyed Isi's outgoing personality, she wasn't sure what Will wanted his family to know about the situation.

"Don't answer that," Isi said. "I didn't mean to pry, but—" her gaze shifted to the door "—the twins' father refused to claim them as his. I didn't find out he was married until I was four months pregnant."

"I'm sorry, Isi."

"I couldn't have picked a better father for my sons than Conway. We're lucky he loves us."

"I'm glad it worked out for you." Marsha stared at the inside of her coffee cup. "How did your parents take the news that you were marrying a Cash brother?"

The light dimmed in Isi's eyes. "My mother and father are deceased and so are my twin brothers. I'm all that remains of my immediate family, but I know in my heart my parents would have approved of Conway."

"What about Aimee Cash and the fact that all her sons were fathered by different men?"

"Does that bother you?" Isi asked.

"No, but my father isn't as understanding."

"Aimee's lifestyle turned a lot of heads in Stagecoach and of course you know better than me because you went to school with the Cash brothers, but I hear they took a lot of ribbing about their names."

"I'm hoping my father eventually comes around but…"

"But what?"

Marsha couldn't believe she was confiding in a practical stranger who wasn't familiar with her and Will's past relationship—if you could call a date to the prom a relationship—but Isi genuinely cared about the Cash family and Marsha sensed she could trust her. "My father's concerned that Will might replace him in my son's affections."

"Then we have to show the pastor that there's enough room in Ryan's life for him, Will and the rest of the Cash family."

"And how do we do that?" Marsha asked.

"For starters we'll have a cookout this afternoon. Once your father gets to know all Will's brothers and what great men they are, he'll relax his guard."

"A barbecue sounds nice," Marsha said.

"I'll tell Conway what we have planned and he'll contact his sister and brothers, then you and I will cook up a storm."

Marsha clanked her cup against Isi's. "I like you, Isi. You're easy to talk to."

"Conway thinks so, too." Isi grabbed a cookbook off the counter and set it in front of Marsha. "Page through this and pick a few recipes that sound good while I check the pantry for supplies."

WILL EYED THE DOGHOUSE and shook his head. He'd built the damn thing for a dog who'd hijacked his day with his son. Ryan and the twins had disappeared over an hour ago and Marsha had yet to come outside after going into the house with Isi.

"Finished?"

Will faced the pastor. "Debating whether or not to add an overhang off the front for shade."

"Might come in handy if the dog rests his head outside the opening."

"Where's Ryan? Maybe he could help me with it," Will said.

"He's on the front porch with the twins, showing them the books on his Kindle."

"Ryan can't go anywhere without that damned thing." As soon as he spoke the words, Will realized his mistake.

The pastor's eyes narrowed. "Are you opposed to reading or just education in general?"

The slap in the face, although deserved, sent Will reeling. It was bad enough that he only possessed a high-school diploma when the mother of his son had earned a doctoral degree. "All I'm saying is that there's more to living than burying your head in a book."

The pastor nodded to the bunkhouse. "What exactly has all that worldly experience gained you?"

Will braced himself for an argument that had been fourteen years in the making. The pastor had never been able to give Will a piece of his mind because Marsha had kept Will's identity a secret up until now. Like any protective father the pastor felt justified in knocking Will down a peg or two for getting his daughter pregnant.

"You and your brothers don't know the value of an education."

In self-defense, Will lashed out. "Book learning is great but man's inventions would be useless without workers to build them."

The pastor nodded as if conceding a point to Will. "College isn't right for everyone, but it is right for Ryan. I better not ever hear that you tried to talk my grandson out of earning a higher degree. I don't want you glamorizing construction work, rodeos or whatever else you do for fun."

Earning the pastor's approval was essential if Will intended to establish a healthy relationship with Ryan. His son idolized his grandfather and if he hoped to earn Ryan's respect, he first had to earn the pastor's.

"Ryan has the right to make his own decisions about his future. If he asks why I didn't go to college, I'll tell him that a person can learn a lot from books and teachers, but until you do the work yourself—like pound nails and saw boards—you'll never appreciate how complex and remarkable something as simple as a house is."

The old man stared long and hard at Will, then nodded. "Let's put the overhang on."

"You don't have to help."

"Are you kidding?" The pastor chuckled. "After that speech you gave? Pass me a board."

Still rattled by their conversation, Will secured the first piece of wood to the roofline while the pastor held it in place. After he nailed the final board, both men admired the structure. "That's a fine doghouse," the pastor said.

"Needs a coat of paint, which the boys can do."

Right then a convoy of pickups pulled into the yard and Will's brothers piled out of their vehicles.

"Heard we were having a barbecue this afternoon," Mack said.

Porter waved. "Johnny and Shannon will be here later."

"Looks like you guys got Isi's message." Conway approached the group.

This was the first Will had heard about a family barbecue. His brothers gathered in front of the doghouse. "I don't know if you've met my brothers...."

"If I have, it's been a while," the pastor said.

Conway held out his hand. "I'm Conway."

Porter and Mack shook hands with the pastor, then a stilted silence settled over the group.

"Let's fire up the grill," Conway said.

His brothers walked off and when Mack spoke, Porter laughed then Conway took a swing at Porter, which led to a scuffle before they disappeared from sight.

"Your brothers get along well," the pastor said.

"We may all have different fathers, but you won't find a tighter-knit group than the Cash brothers." As soon as he said the words an image of Buck popped into his mind. Some brother Will was—banishing Buck from the family fold.

MARSHA SAT AT the picnic table in the backyard, listening to her father sing "Swing Low, Sweet Chariot" while Mack strummed his guitar. Will, Porter, Conway and their brother-in-law, Gavin, threw the football to each other while Ryan sat on the porch reading to the twins on his Kindle. Marsha couldn't tell Javier and Miguel apart but one of them appeared fascinated by the e-reader and the other's attention kept wandering to his uncles. Bandit slept in the shade beneath the picnic table where the women sat and Dixie pushed her sleeping son, Nate, in the baby swing.

Everyone was accounted for except Buck and Marsha was surprised he hadn't come to the picnic. Was he angry she hadn't told Will about Ryan when he'd guessed the truth over a year ago?

"It's too bad your mother couldn't join us," Isi said, during a lull in conversation.

"She would have enjoyed meeting all of you." Marsha nodded to the baby. "Especially little Nate."

"Is she not feeling well?" Shannon asked.

"My mother plays bridge on Saturday afternoons with a group of ladies from the church." Marsha smiled when Mack switched to a jumpy tune and her father clapped his hands along with the music. "Mack has won my father over with his guitar playing."

"Mack wins everyone over with his talent," Dixie said.

Shannon rubbed her belly and winced.

"What's wrong?" Dixie asked.

"I'm uncomfortable. This baby can't arrive soon enough."

"When are you due?" Marsha asked.

"Yesterday."

Marsha winced. "I was two weeks overdue with Ryan."

"Must have been difficult going through a pregnancy alone," Dixie said. The tone of her voice sounded innocent enough, but the steely light in her gaze said she wasn't happy that Marsha had kept Ryan away from their family.

No matter how Marsha bent her rationale to fit her actions, she couldn't deny how unfair she'd been to Will.

He might have screwed up, but he'd been young and as frightened as her when she'd found out she was pregnant. Yes, he'd admitted he didn't want a baby, but in the end, she was the one who hadn't told him that she was keeping their child.

"Ryan seems like a nice boy," Isi said. "The twins love him."

The compliments made Marsha feel even worse.

"When Conway gave Bandit to the boys, I thought our family was set, but Javier accosted me in the kitchen earlier and said he wants a big brother."

"From now on Ryan will be their big brother." Dixie placed a tray of fresh veggies between the women.

"I heard you opened a gift shop in Yuma," Marsha said.

"Dixie's Desert Delights," Dixie said. "I sell homemade bath soaps and other girlie stuff."

"You should stop in," Shannon said. "The soap recipes belong to Grandma Ada's family."

"How interesting." Marsha realized how little she knew about Will's family.

"Isi emigrated from Buenos Aires when she was eighteen," Dixie said.

"Really? Three years ago I took a group of physics students to the World Science Fair there. I thought Buenos Aires was such a romantic city with its European architecture and theaters."

"I rarely saw the nice areas of the city," Isi said. "I grew up in La Boca. My mother's great-grandparents emigrated from Spain to Argentina. My father's relatives are native Argentineans."

"Will said you're a teacher." Dixie spoke to Marsha.

"I teach high-school chemistry. This summer I'm

tutoring physics students online for the University of California, Los Angeles."

"You must have gotten your master's degree then?" Isi asked.

Marsha didn't bother adding that she'd also earned a doctoral degree.

Isi rolled her eyes. "And here I was proud of myself for earning an AA degree from the community college."

"Is it true that Conway took over the pecan farm?" Marsha asked.

Dixie laughed. "Who would have believed the local Casanova had a love for tractors and pecan trees."

"Hey, ladies!" Porter yelled. "Bring your plates over here. The burgers are done."

"I'll get your food, Dad." Marsha stopped next to his chair.

"I may be old, daughter, but I can carry a paper plate."

Properly chastened, Marsha waited for him to stand, then walked with him to the grill. When he stumbled, Mack stepped forward and steadied him.

"Whoa, there, cowboy. Are you sure you didn't drink that beer Will offered you?" Mack asked.

Her father chuckled. "You Cash boys always were smart-alecky."

The comment kicked off a half hour of Cash brother good-old-days stories. As she listened to the men talk, her eyes strayed to Will, who stood in front of the porch. He spoke to the twins and they laughed. Ryan ignored him. Marsha hoped the others hadn't noticed her son's rudeness. When Will joined his brothers by the grill, Marsha sat on the porch steps with the boys. "Bandit has a pretty nice doghouse, don't you think?"

"Uncle Will's the best builder in the whole world," Miguel said.

Marsha glanced at Ryan to gauge his reaction but he focused on his food.

Javier patted Marsha's leg to get her attention. "And my dad's the best farmer in the whole world."

"He's my dad, too." Miguel nudged his brother, and Javier's plate almost tumbled to the ground.

"Hey, fighting's not cool," Ryan said.

The twins gaped at their older cousin then Miguel mumbled, "Sorry."

Javier shrugged. "That's okay."

Marsha caught Ryan smiling at the boys and she sensed that he liked being idolized by the twins. Her son hadn't helped Will build the doghouse, but the day had gone better than she'd expected. She listened to the twins tell the story of how Conway used to be their babysitter before he became their father and the love in their voices gave Marsha hope that Ryan and Will would find their way as father and son, too.

"Care to go for a walk?" Will asked when he approached the porch.

Miguel set his plate aside and stood. "Where are we goin', Uncle Will?"

"Not you, Mig," Ryan said. "He's asking my mom to go for a walk."

"Oh." Miguel sat down and shoveled a forkful of baked beans into his mouth.

"You're welcome to come, too, Ryan…if you want," Will said.

Javier nudged Ryan's leg. "Stay here."

"Looks like you've got a new fan club," Will said.

"Ryan's a good reader, Uncle Will." Javier smiled

at his cousin. "He's reading us *Harry Potter* on his computer."

"It's an e-reader," Ryan said.

"Yeah, his e-reader," Javier repeated.

"I'll stay," Ryan said.

As Marsha left the backyard with Will she caught her father watching them. She expected he'd have a lot to say after spending the day at the Cash farm.

## Chapter Seven

Once Marsha and Will were out of view of their families, she asked, "Are you upset about today?"

"What do you mean?"

"You got stuck building the doghouse by yourself and my father tagged along for the day." She smiled. "Feel free to vent."

Will stopped walking. "Am I free to vent or will whatever I say about Ryan and your father be used against me?"

"Did something happen today that I don't know about?"

He opened his mouth then snapped it shut. "You want to see the pond or not?"

She clutched his shirtsleeve, before he took a step. "Wait." His muscles tensed, but he didn't pull away. "I want this to work out for you and Ryan."

"Do you?"

She bristled but held her tongue.

"Or are you hoping I'll make mistakes, so Ryan will want nothing to do with me?"

"I can't believe you'd think that."

"Why not? If things don't work out for me and Ryan, you head back to California with a clear conscience."

The brown eyes staring at her were filled with pain and shame swept through Marsha. She expected that this father-son reunion would be difficult, but her main concern had been for Ryan's emotional well-being. She hadn't given much thought to the turmoil Will might be feeling. "I'll do everything in my power to help you both, but you'll have to communicate with me. I can't read your mind."

Will stared into space. "We're strangers who made a baby."

"Then why don't we get reacquainted," she said.

His rigid posture relaxed. "We're pouring the cement slab for the classroom hallway Wednesday afternoon and Ben and I had planned to take Thursday off while the cement dries."

"I'm free after 10:00 a.m."

"What do you want to do?" he asked.

"Surprise me." Marsha followed Will past the barn and down the path that led to a pond. "This is nice." A pecan tree next to the water provided shade from the sun. "Did you build the pier?"

Will nodded. "Conway wanted to teach the twins how to swim and dive."

"The water's deep enough for diving?"

"Yep, and it's stocked with carp and catfish."

Marsha yearned to sit beneath the tree with Will— the young girl who'd been infatuated with the bad boy would love to taste his kiss again. "I'd better take my father home. It's been a long day for him."

Will's gaze mesmerized Marsha and she couldn't have moved her feet if she'd wanted to. His brown eyes warmed as he zeroed in on her lips—maybe she'd get her wish after all and Will would kiss her.

No such luck. He spun and led the way back to the house.

Marsha walked at his side, noticing how careful he was not to brush against her. "Where was Buck today?" she asked.

Will's step faltered. "He's gone."

"Gone where?"

"He left town."

His curt answer surprised her. "Did Buck say when he'd return?"

The barn came into view and Will slowed his steps. "Buck and I had words. We both needed time to cool off."

The Buck she knew never instigated an argument. "Words about what?"

"Leave it alone, Marsha."

*Great.* Will and Buck had quarreled over her and Ryan. Her decision to keep Ryan a secret for so long was causing more collateral damage than she could have ever imagined.

MARSHA STARED AT her outfit in the mirror attached to the back of the bedroom door—a yellow sundress with strappy white sandals. It wasn't that long ago that she'd preened in front of the same mirror, wearing a prom dress and imagining Will kissing her good-night. A tender ache spread through her chest when she thought of what she and Will had done in his grandfather's pickup.

"Honey, Will's here." Her mother opened Marsha's door and poked her head inside the room. "You look nice."

"Thanks." Marsha removed a white cardigan sweater from the closet—in case Will liked to blast the air-conditioning in his truck. "Did Dad grumble about me going off with Will today?" Strangely enough her father hadn't uttered one negative comment about the Cash family after spending the previous Saturday at their farm.

"No, but he did tell me how much he enjoyed getting to know Will's family."

"Really? He said that?"

"Not in those exact words." Her mother smiled. "He said things like… 'Conway's sons are cute little buggers'. And 'Mack's voice sure is easy on the ears. He should sing in our church choir'."

"What did he say about Will?"

"Nothing, but Ryan mentioned that Will built the doghouse in record time."

Not much of a compliment as far as Marsha was concerned. Hopefully that would change after father and son became more comfortable with each other.

"Remind me again why you and Will are going out?" her mother said.

Her parents were protective of her—especially her father. He feared she'd slip under Will's spell again. She wished she could reassure him she wouldn't, but Will still possessed his bad-boy aura from high school and her heart raced whenever he looked at her. "Will has a lot of questions about Ryan."

"Will's a handsome man and you're both young. Sharing a child is a strong bond."

Marsha sat on the bed and patted the mattress beside her. Once her mother joined her, she said, "I know you think I'll get my heart broken again."

"Did Will break your heart all those years ago?"

"Yes, but in his defense, he never led me on. I'd had

a crush on him my senior year." And up until today....
"I haven't gone on a date in forever, Mom."

"Is this a real date?"

Marsha's emotional side hoped so—her intellectual
side...not so much. "I'm not sure."

"What do you have in common with Will besides..."
Her mother's cheeks turned pink.

"Why all these questions, Mom?"

"I've never spoken about this—not even to your father." She wrung her hands. "The reason you were adopted is because *I* couldn't have children."

What did this have to do with her and Will? "I assumed it was either you or Dad who was sterile."

"I wasn't always sterile, honey."

"What happened?"

"I became pregnant when I was fifteen."

Marsha swallowed a gasp.

"I was too terrified to tell my parents, because the
young man who got me pregnant was a deacon in the
church." She sniffed. "He was handsome and outside
of church he ran with a wild crowd like Will. I believed
I could change him."

Like Marsha had thought she could change Will.
"Did you love him?"

"I did."

"What happened to the baby?"

Tears glistened in her mother's eyes. "The deacon
gave me the number of a doctor who'd take care of me.
He said if I really loved him I'd abort the baby."

"But abortion was illegal in the 1950s." Never mind
that Will waited outside for her, Marsha wasn't budging
until her mother finished her story. "What happened?"

"I called the number and spoke to a woman who

arranged for a car to pick me up on the corner of Euclid and Downing. A mile from my family's apartment. When I got in the car I was told to put on a blindfold. A half hour later the car parked in the driveway of a ranch-style home. I had no idea where we were, but I believe it was the doctor's private residence."

Marsha was horrified her mother had gone alone to get an abortion.

"I was ushered inside, told to take off my panties and get up on the kitchen table, which had been covered with a white sheet."

A lump formed in Marsha's throat and she squeezed her mother's hand.

"It was over in a matter of minutes. He told me to get dressed and that I would start bleeding in a day or two and the cramping would be painful."

"Then the driver dropped you off where he'd picked you up," Marsha said.

"Yes."

"How much did the doctor charge you?"

"A hundred dollars."

A hundred dollars in the '50s had been a fortune. "Where did you get that kind of money?"

Her mother's face burned red. "The deacon stole the money from the donation plates in church."

*Good Lord.*

"I repaid that money. I spent an entire year babysitting and cleaning homes, but the church got every penny back." She wiped a tear. "That was the least of my problems. I started bleeding like the doctor said I would, but it didn't stop. My mother became fearful. She took me to the doctor and he'd known right away what I'd done. As I healed, I developed too much scar tissue to become pregnant."

Marsha's heart ached for her mother. "I'm sorry I didn't tell you when I found out I was pregnant."

"I'm not angry about that, honey. When you'd told us about Ryan after he'd been born, I confess that I felt a huge sense of relief that I didn't know beforehand."

"Why?"

"Because I believe the news would have opened the door to feelings I'd locked away deep inside me and I would have felt the need to confess my past sins to your father."

"Dad doesn't know why you couldn't become pregnant?"

"No. He'd placed all his faith in God and told me that if God wanted me to get pregnant it would happen and if he didn't, it wouldn't."

Marsha understood some of the guilt her mother had lived with, knowing that God had played no role in her ability to become pregnant. And she felt bad that her mother had deceived her father but she was the last person who should judge her mother.

Her father may have his prejudices, but he loved her mother. They had a fulfilling marriage and her mother had been active in helping him in his ministry—she was the perfect pastor's wife. "Why did you marry Dad if you knew you couldn't have children?"

Tears dribbled from her mother's eyes. "I was young and scared and full of guilt. I believed the path to God's forgiveness was marrying a pastor and working by his side."

"Do you love Dad?"

"I didn't when I married him." A dreamy expression filled her mother's eyes. "But it wasn't long before my admiration for him grew into love and now—" her voice wobbled "—I don't know what I'm going to do without him."

Marsha hugged her mother. "It looks like we've both kept a pretty big secret in our lives."

"But you're making things right, honey." Her mother brushed her hand over Marsha's hair. "You're giving Ryan and Will the chance to be father and son."

"I'm sad you couldn't have children yet grateful that God picked you and Dad to be my parents. I love you both." Marsha hugged her mother.

"Where is Will taking you today?"

"He's surprising me."

Her mother went to the door. "After I got the abortion…the deacon wanted nothing to do with me." She sniffed. "Be careful, honey. I learned the hard way that a man will say things you want to hear so he can have his way with you, then he moves on without a backward glance."

Marsha felt terrible that her mother had been used in such a way. "I'm older and wiser, Mom."

"Let's hope your heart as well as your brain was paying attention in all those college classes you took."

"We've made Will wait long enough. I'd better rescue him from Dad." When she stepped outside she spotted her father and Will beneath the carport. "Hi, Will."

"Marsha."

"Drive carefully." Her father hugged her and walked off.

"Is Ryan here?" Will said.

"He hasn't come outside?" That her son had hidden

in the house angered Marsha. She'd taught him better manners. "Give me a second."

Inside the house she called Ryan's name before entering his bedroom. He lay on the bed reading. "Why haven't you gone outside to speak to your father?"

"I'm almost finished with this chapter."

She crossed the room and removed the e-reader from his hand. "You've never been this rude before."

"What does it matter if I say hi to him?" Ryan swung his legs off the bed and sat up. "He doesn't like me."

"Why would you think that?"

"He hardly talked to me at the barbecue."

"You were the one who walked off when he built the doghouse."

"He didn't want my help."

"Did Will tell you that?"

"No, but I know he was angry, because I didn't want to use the nail gun."

"We'll discuss your attitude when I get home tonight." She returned to the carport and said, "I'm afraid Ryan's not feeling well."

Will's stare burned a hole through her dress. "You don't have to lie. He doesn't want to see me, does he?"

Aware of her parents watching through the window, she said, "Let's talk about this on the way to wherever it is we're going today." She hopped into the front seat and less than a minute later, Will turned the truck onto the highway and headed south away from Stagecoach.

"So...where are we going?"

Will expelled a frustrated breath, then relaxed his grip on the wheel. "I thought we'd drive toward Ajo." He breathed in the sweet scent of Marsha's perfume.

The last female who'd sat this close to him had been Isi when he'd taken her on a date as a favor to Conway. The physical attraction hadn't been there between them, but they'd enjoyed talking to each other and as a result had become friends. He was comfortable with Isi, because he felt her equal—he couldn't say the same for Marsha.

"There's a restaurant called the Devil's Plateau that serves great steaks," he said. "It's built at the top of a mesa near Ajo. The panoramic view of the desert is pretty impressive."

"Sounds nice."

He hoped to impress her with the restaurant—he'd worn his newest pair of jeans and dress boots. He assumed Marsha was used to upscale eateries in California, whereas he preferred the food found in desert dives along the highway.

He squirmed in his seat, wracking his brain for a conversation starter. Funny how he hadn't been the least bit nervous when he'd coaxed a much younger Marsha into the backseat of his grandfather's pickup.

In an effort to redirect his thoughts he asked, "What do you like most about teaching?"

"The kids, of course." She shifted toward him. "It amazes me how smart my students are."

"How many science classes do you teach a day?"

"Four, and one is an AP course."

At the risk of sounding stupid, he asked, "What does AP stand for?"

"Advanced placement. The classes are college level and if the student's passing score is high enough on the comprehensive exam at the end of the semester, then they earn college credit for the course." She waved a hand in the air. "There's a big push by parents for schools to offer more AP courses, because it saves on tuition costs down the road. I've seen kids accumulate enough AP credits to begin college as sophomores instead of freshmen."

"Is Ryan taking any AP courses?"

"Next year, he'll be in two classes."

"Which ones?"

"Biology and English."

When Will had been a sophomore, all he'd thought about was girls. "Are you sure it's smart to push him so hard?"

She stiffened. "I'm not pushing him. I'm restraining him."

"What do you mean?"

"I had Ryan tested a couple of years ago."

"Tested for what?"

"His IQ."

With Marsha for a mother, Will assumed his son would be bright. "How smart is he?"

"His IQ score two years ago was 144."

"Is that high enough to be considered a genius?"

"Not quite, but it's close."

Will's stomach bottomed out. No wonder Ryan had snubbed his nose at building a doghouse. If Will had suggested they construct a nuclear generator, Ryan would have been over-the-moon excited.

"Can I ask you a personal question?"

He braced himself. "Sure."

"Do you know much about your father or his side of the family? Was he a professional? Maybe a doctor?"

The fact that she'd skipped over him and assumed their son might have inherited his high IQ from a relative of Will's, tweaked his pride. "I know very little about my birth father." Only that the man was a cruel bastard.

"Have you ever had your IQ tested?" she asked.

Will laughed—the sound a harsh bark, not a heart-felt chuckle.

"I know you didn't apply yourself in school," Marsha said. "But a lot of high IQ kids don't, because they're bored in class."

Will might as well set Marsha straight, but he hated discussing his handicap. When he'd been sent to the special-education center in elementary school, he'd convinced his friends that he was being punished because he refused to do his class assignments—not because he had trouble reading. He was tempted to lie to Marsha, but lies had gotten them into their current situation. "I was diagnosed with dyslexia in third grade."

"Really?" Marsha frowned. "You hid it well."

"So now you know that Ryan couldn't have inherited his intelligence from me. He must have gotten his genes from your side of the family."

"Will, dyslexia has nothing to do with intelligence. Besides, I wouldn't know if Ryan inherited his smarts from my side of the family."

"How come?"

"You never heard?" she asked.

"Heard what?"

"That I'm adopted."

Shocked, he gaped at her. "I had no idea."

"I don't talk about it much, but my close friends in school knew."

"Have you kept in touch with your birth parents?" he asked.

"They're dead. I lived with them until I was two, but I don't remember them."

"What happened?"

"My parents were drug-addicted teenagers. One day a neighbor called the police and reported a toddler walking in the parking lot of the apartment complex wearing only a diaper. When the police arrived, they found my parents dead from a drug overdose inside the apartment."

"You had no relatives to take you in?"

"No one came forward to claim me."

Will's mother had come and gone through the years, but his grandparents had always been there for him and his siblings. "Considering what happened to you, I'm surprised you didn't go through with the abortion."

"I was raised in a religious home. Abortion wasn't an option."

Will hadn't sorted through all his feelings about Marsha keeping Ryan a secret and thought it best to keep his thoughts to himself lest he ruin their afternoon together. "You must like teaching, because it gives you summers off," he said, changing the subject.

"I never take the summers off. I usually teach summer school, but since I'm spending almost three months in Stagecoach, I took a job as an online tutor for the UCLA science department. I'd like to work as a professor at UCLA so I can earn more money."

"Do you have a lot of student-loan debt?"

"Not really. I was on full scholarship my first four years of college, then I received a grant, which paid for my master's degree. My doctoral degree was expensive and I haven't paid off those loans yet."

"Did your parents help you financially after you had Ryan?"

"Yes, but I wish I wouldn't have taken their money."

"Why's that?"

"Because they used up most of their retirement savings fighting Dad's cancer and there's little left for Mom to live on after he passes away."

While Marsha coped with all her responsibilities, Will went about his day-to-day activities only caring for himself. Had one of the reasons she'd kept Ryan a secret from him been that she believed she couldn't count on him for financial support? A pit formed in the bottom of Will's stomach when he recalled his father's shadowy image standing behind the door. Will couldn't decide which rejection hurt the most—his father's or Marsha's.

What had happened in the past was done. Finished. Over. None of them got a redo. From here on out Will was determined to find a way to earn his son's respect and maybe Marsha's, too. "Did Ryan enjoy hanging out at the farm?"

"He wouldn't stop talking about Javier, Miguel and Bandit," she said. "Ryan loves dogs, but with both of us at school, I didn't think it was fair to own an animal and leave it alone all day."

Maybe Will could win Ryan over if he bought him a dog. It had worked for Conway.

"Don't even think about it," Marsha said, as if she'd read his mind.

"The dog could live with me and when Ryan visits—"

"That's a generous offer, Will, but Ryan's going to be focusing more and more on building his résumé for college and depending on what activities he becomes involved in, he may or may not have time to travel to Stagecoach in the summer."

Will choked the steering wheel and pulled off the road, then shifted into Park. He couldn't believe Marsha would tell him he had a son after all these years and then not give him an opportunity to be with Ryan. "What good will it do to connect with Ryan if you two never come back to Stagecoach?"

"You can't expect us to drop everything in our lives, so we can spend summers here, while you go about working your construction jobs?"

He swallowed his anger, grudgingly admiring the way she stood up to him. The spark in her eyes ignited a slow burn in his gut and suddenly he found himself leaning across the seat. "I'm going to kiss you."

"Okay." The word escaped her mouth in a whisper of air that caressed his cheek.

He angled his head and brushed his mouth against hers. His first thought was how soft her lips felt. He slid his fingers through her hair, holding her head while he deepened the kiss. She tasted sweet and hot all at once and he couldn't get enough of her taste and scent. He moved his hand to her hip then up along her rib cage to her—

His cell phone beeped, startling them apart.

"Aren't you going to check the text?" she asked in a husky voice.

The spell had been broken. Will released Marsha and looked at his phone. "It's from Johnny," he said. "Shannon went into labor. They're heading to the hospital in Yuma."

Any plans to pick up where they'd left off had died a

quick death. "My niece or nephew has rotten timing." He texted Johnny that he was on the way to the hospital, then made a U-turn. "I'm sorry about lunch, but family comes first."

Marsha was awfully quiet during the drive to Yuma and Will suspected that didn't bode well for the kiss they'd shared.

## Chapter Eight

"Did I make it in time?" Will said when he entered the waiting room of the maternity ward at the Yuma Medical Center where his brothers had gathered.

Marsha hung back, not wanting to intrude on the family moment.

"They took Shannon into the delivery room," Porter said. He glanced behind Will. "Hey, Marsha."

"Hello." She sat in the chair nearest the door.

Conway's gaze swung between Will and Marsha and she hoped her mouth wasn't swollen from the kiss Will had given her a short while ago. She'd been so flustered she hadn't touched up her lipstick before entering the hospital.

"Where were you going when Johnny texted you?" Conway asked.

"Ajo," Will said.

Mack pointed to Will's mouth and grinned.

"What?"

"When did you start wearing pink lipstick?" Mack chuckled and the rest of the Cash brothers hooted.

Embarrassed, Marsha felt her face warm.

"Knock it off, Mack," Will warned. "Where's Clive and Shannon's brothers?"

"Shannon's dad left Phoenix an hour ago, but I don't think he'll make it in time and Matt and Luke are in court today," Conway said.

The waiting-room door opened and Johnny stepped inside, wearing a green surgical gown. He wasn't smiling.

Marsha's embarrassment forgotten, her stomach tightened.

"What's wrong?" Will grabbed Johnny's arm.

"The doctor said Shannon's not dilating fast enough and the baby's in distress."

The room swelled with a nervous silence.

"Where's Dixie?" Johnny asked. "Shannon wants her."

Porter stepped forward. "She was at the farm with Isi when we called her."

"She should be here by now." Johnny paced the floor.

"This is Dixie," Conway said, checking a text on his phone.

"When's she getting here?" Johnny asked.

Marsha's heart went out to the father-to-be. The Cash brothers had been larger-than-life teenage fantasies in high school, but seeing them interact with each other in a crisis proved they were as human and vulnerable as the next person.

Conway glanced up from his phone, his face pale. "A tire blew on Dixie's car as she was pulling out of the driveway. She thinks she drove over a screw."

Johnny gaped. "You're kidding?"

Will grimaced. "Damn. I might have dropped a screw or nail when I made the doghouse. I'm sorry, Johnny."

"Can't Isi give her a ride into Yuma?" Porter asked.

Conway shook his head. "Isi's car is at Troy Winters's garage having the carburetor replaced."

Will reached for the door handle. "I'll get Dixie."

"There's no time," Johnny said.

Marsha stood, her heart pounding fiercely. "I'll talk to Shannon."

Johnny shook his head. "Thanks, Marsha, but—"

"Ryan was born by cesarean section." She glanced at Will, noting his surprised gaze before he stared out the window overlooking the parking lot. She hated that he had to learn about Ryan's birth in front of his brothers.

"Follow me." Johnny held the door open for her. "Thank you. Shannon will appreciate the support."

Outside in the hallway Marsha said, "She's going to be okay, Johnny."

"I thought watching her come out of the chute on two thousand pounds of raging bull was scary, but this is a lot worse."

They stopped at the nurses' station where he introduced Marsha. The nurse gave her a gown, cap and gloves to put on, then told Johnny she'd get him a fresh gown after she escorted Marsha into the operating room.

"Shannon, Marsha's here," the nurse said. "Johnny will be back in a minute."

When Marsha saw the tears in Shannon's eyes, she offered an encouraging smile.

"Is Dixie coming?" Shannon asked.

"She had a flat tire and she and Isi are stranded at the farm. Will got the call you'd gone into labor while we were on our way to Ajo." She squeezed Shannon's hand, but when she attempted to let go, Shannon clung to her fingers.

"I don't want to have a cesarean," she said. "I can do this on my own."

"I had Ryan by cesarean," Marsha said.

Shannon's eyes widened.

"And I was terrified."

"Why did your doctor perform a cesarean?"

"Ryan's head was too large to fit through the birth canal."

Shannon's grip on Marsha's hand tightened. "The doctor said the baby's heartbeat is slowing."

"Trust your doctor, Shannon."

"What if they hurt the baby?"

Marsha's pulse raced at the sound of panic in Shannon's voice. "They'll be very careful." She'd felt the same helplessness when she'd run into complications delivering Ryan—only she'd been all alone in the delivery room.

*That's because you chose not to tell Will or your parents.*

"How painful is the recovery?" Shannon asked.

"For a woman who once rode bulls—" Marsha smiled behind her surgical mask "—a walk in the park."

Johnny appeared on the opposite side of the operating table and held his wife's hand.

"Are we ready to have this baby?" the doctor asked.

Shannon released her grip on Marsha's fingers. "Thank you."

"I'll let you two experience this amazing miracle together." Marsha made a hasty escape, not wanting Johnny or Shannon to see the tears in her eyes. Outside the delivery room she leaned against the wall and willed her pounding heart to slow down.

The consequences of her actions in high school had

hit her full force when she'd walked into the delivery room—she'd denied Will the opportunity to see his son born. Yes, he'd insisted she have an abortion and maybe he wouldn't have wanted to be with her during the delivery, but it had been his choice to make—not hers.

She removed her gloves, mask and gown and tossed them into a hamper by the door, then returned to the waiting room, where Mack told her that Will had gone to the cafeteria. After reassuring the brothers that Shannon would be fine, she went in search of Will and found him sitting in the shade on the patio.

"Mind if I join you?" she asked when she approached his table.

Will used his boot to push the chair out across from him. "How's Shannon?"

"Scared." She sat then waited for Will to speak. He didn't, so she brought up the subject that was on both their minds. "Everything was going fine with my pregnancy until two weeks before my delivery date."

Will remained silent—he wasn't going to let her off easy.

"The ultrasound showed Ryan's head was too large to fit through the birth canal." She tried to lighten the mood. "You know what they say...smart kids and jocks all have big heads."

Will didn't crack a smile. "Your parents must have been worried."

"They didn't know I was pregnant. They learned about Ryan when they visited me in California the summer after he was born."

"You went through the whole pregnancy alone?" he asked.

Her eyes stung when she recalled Johnny holding

Shannon's hand in the operating room. "I believed I was doing the right thing."

"And now?" His voice sounded rusty.

"I wish you'd have been there to hold my hand through the operation."

Will pushed his chair out and stood. "Walk with me." They strolled across the patio to a bench which had more privacy. There wasn't much room for one person on the seat, never mind two.

A tingle spread through her thigh where it rubbed against Will's leg. Her physical attraction to him had never been an issue—actually she'd developed a bad habit of comparing the few men she'd dated to Will. She'd never been able to shake his bad-boy image from her memory and even now he projected an aura of approach-at-your-own-risk, which excited her.

Before she got too carried away with her thoughts, she asked the question that had been on her mind since arriving in Stagecoach. "What happened between you and Buck? I feel terrible that you two had a falling-out."

Leaning forward, Will clasped his hands between his knees. "We got into a fight over you."

"There's never been anything remotely romantic between me and Buck. We're just friends."

"He said that." Will's gaze glanced off her. "Buck should have told me over a year ago that Ryan was my son and not promised you he'd keep your secret."

Marsha felt horrible that she'd come between the brothers. "I wonder how things would have worked out for everyone, if I'd raised Ryan in Stagecoach."

"That was never an option, was it?" Will asked.

She shook her head. "I knew if I didn't leave town, I'd never go to college."

"What do you think you would have done, if you'd stayed?"

"I'd have become involved in my father's church and probably would have taught Sunday-school classes."

She shuddered as she recalled the feelings she'd struggled with as a teenager. Since she and Will had opened this discussion, she wanted to be totally honest with him. "I was scared to death when I found out I was pregnant with Ryan."

"And I was scared out of my mind when you told me," Will said.

"I almost went through with an abortion."

"What stopped you?"

"My conscience. The longer I sat in the waiting room the more excuses I came up with for keeping my baby."

"Like what?"

"For one, I didn't want to disappoint my father or mother."

"Then why not tell them that you were pregnant?" Will asked.

"I believed my father would make trouble for you. And since I was the one who kept saying it was okay when you tried to stop…."

Will reached for her hand. "If anyone was to blame, Marsha, it was me. I knew better not to have sex without a condom."

"You offered to stop, but I wouldn't let you. Remember?"

He grinned. "You were impatient."

She nodded, feeling light-headed with relief now that she'd confessed to Will.

"Right now I'm wishing you had remained in Stagecoach. Who knows, maybe I would have gotten used to the idea of being a father. We might not have married, but I could have been there for Ryan."

"I've thought about that plenty, Will, but it would never have happened."

"What do you mean?"

"My father would have intervened and made you miserable until you agreed to keep your distance from me and Ryan."

"Your father has never thought highly of me or my brothers."

"No, he hasn't, but old age has mellowed him."

"What was your parents' reaction when they saw Ryan?"

"My father was disappointed that I'd gotten pregnant out of wedlock but proud of me for having the courage to keep the baby. Mom was thrilled to be a grandma."

"They didn't demand you reveal the identity of Ryan's father?"

"They nagged me for months then finally quit when I showed them I could manage school and raise Ryan on my own. I took him to the campus day care when I was in class."

"Were you afraid I'd try to take Ryan away from you, if you'd told me after he was born?"

"That never crossed my mind."

"Then why didn't you contact me? You've had more than enough time to find a way to tell me I was a father."

She'd often envisioned herself having this conversation with Will but had never imagined him being this calm or reasonable. The Will Cash sitting next to her wasn't the same guy she'd gone to the prom with. He'd changed. Matured. Grown up. And he deserved the truth no matter how bad it made her look.

"I was selfish," she said. "I wanted to earn a master's degree, then a doctorate. After I'd graduated with a B.S. in chemistry, I was offered a teaching internship at UCLA. I thought if I'd told you about Ryan, we'd end up in court fighting over shared custody and—"

"I'd ruin your plans."

"I did what I felt was best."

"For you. Not for Ryan or for me."

"For me and for Ryan." She held Will's gaze. "Have you ever met Hillary Bancroft? She was a friend of mine in high school."

"I know who she is," Will said. "She works at the hair salon in Stagecoach."

"I kept in touch with Hillary through the years and she—"

"Told you what I was up to?"

Darn, he was good at finishing her thoughts. "I was waiting for you to settle down and find a stable job, but you were rodeoing and…"

"Chasing after girls."

Marsha nodded. "So I focused on my own career, knowing I'd be the one supporting Ryan and paying for his college."

Marsha's words smacked Will hard and his chest felt as if it had caved in. "You never gave me a chance to prove myself. Had I known about Ryan I would have quit rodeo and found a decent job, so I could pay child support." His words sounded confident, but Will wasn't sure he'd have come through for Marsha. Back then, he'd been a hell-raiser and more concerned with partying than figuring out what he wanted to do with his life.

"I don't resent you for the choices you've made," she said. "We are who we are."

He gaped at her. "What's that supposed to mean?"

There was sympathy in her eyes when she smiled at him. "You're thirty-two and you live in a bunkhouse with your brothers."

The muscle along his jaw knotted and she must have sensed she'd offended him because she said, "There's nothing wrong with the way you live. I'm saying that maybe things worked out for the best."

"For the daughter of a pastor who spent her fair share of hours inside a church, you don't have much faith in people, do you?"

She gasped.

Will shot off the bench and walked away then stopped and faced her. "I can't change the past, but I intend to show you that there's more to Will Cash than what meets the eye." His phone beeped and he scanned the text from Porter. "Shannon had the baby."

In silence, he and Marsha rode the elevator to the maternity ward. When they entered the waiting room, his brothers were passing out pink-labeled cigars.

Mack grinned. "It's a girl."

"Nate's not going to like having to play dolls with his new cousin," Will said. The brothers chuckled. "Have they named her yet?"

"They're naming her Ada for Grandma and for Dixie's little girl," Conway said.

"Dixie's okay with that?" Will asked. He turned to Marsha and said quietly, "Dixie lost her baby daughter before she and Gavin had Nate."

Porter nodded. "Shannon and Dixie talked about it before the baby was born."

"Anybody get a hold of Buck and tell him?" Will asked.

Porter shook his head. "We left messages on his phone, but he hasn't responded to any of our calls." The brothers swung their gazes toward Marsha and her face paled.

"When can we see the baby?" Will asked.

"Right now." Johnny waltzed into the room, wearing a smile, but looking as if he'd gone ten rounds with a rank bronc.

"Congratulations, big brother," Mack said, patting Johnny's shoulder.

"Yeah, how does it feel to be a daddy?" Conway asked.

Before Johnny spoke, Porter said, "You're the first of us brothers to have a baby and it's only fitting it was a girl seeing how close you've always been to Dixie."

Will stood in stunned silence, listening to his brothers. It was as if they'd forgotten all about Will being a father. Out of the corner of his eye he saw Marsha duck from the room.

Conway jabbed his fist into Mack's shoulder. "I bet you're gonna be a father next."

"No, way. I'm staying single for a while."

"Yeah, well don't wait too long or Nate and my daughter will be too old to play with your kids," Johnny said. "C'mon, I'll show you where the nursery is. Little Addy has a ton of black hair."

The brothers turned toward the door, then froze when they saw Will. "Congratulations, Johnny." Will took off—the last thing he wanted to see was his baby niece through a nursery window, knowing he'd been robbed of that moment with Ryan.

*You might have missed Ryan's birth but that doesn't mean you can't experience other firsts with your son.*

The voice in his head soothed Will's tortured soul and when he reached the lobby and found Marsha waiting for him, he'd decided that no one would rob him of his right to be a father.

FRIDAY MARSHA WOKE to construction sounds—saws and hammering. She trudged into the bathroom, took a shower, then applied her makeup and dressed for the day. She'd grab a quick breakfast before she logged on to the university website and tutored math students the rest of the morning.

When she entered the kitchen, her parents had already eaten and her father's head was buried in the newspaper. Marsha poured herself a cup of coffee and sat at the table.

"You haven't said much about your lunch with Will yesterday." Her mother set a banana and a bowl of cereal in front of Marsha.

"Thanks, Mom." She ate her cereal, feeling her father's penetrating gaze through the newspaper. "Our lunch got interrupted."

"Oh?" her mother said.

"Johnny's wife went into labor and we drove to the hospital to wait for her to have the baby."

"What did Shannon have?" her mother asked.

"A little girl. They named her Ada after the brothers' grandmother." She expected a comment from her father, but his face remained hidden behind the paper.

She'd had hours to think last night, because sleep had eluded her. She acknowledged that there was nothing she could do to make up for keeping Ryan and Will apart, but from here on out she could guarantee that Will had opportunities to be with his son—beginning today.

Ryan stumbled into the kitchen, rubbing his eyes. "How come they're making so much noise?" He removed a box of his favorite cereal from the pantry then a bowl from the cupboard. Ryan wasn't a morning person—he claimed his brain didn't turn on until lunchtime.

"It's hot in Arizona, in case you haven't noticed." She ruffled his hair and he groaned. "Construction workers like to start early before the heat of the day settles in."

"Do we have any plans later?" Ryan asked.

"Nope. I'm working this morning," Marsha said. "You can hang out and do whatever you want until Will finishes for the day."

Ryan's head jerked toward her at the same time her father folded over the corner of the newspaper and stared.

"Why does it matter when Will quits working?" Ryan asked.

"I thought it would be nice if you spent the weekend with your dad."

Ryan's eyes rounded and she braced herself for an argument.

"I don't want to spend the weekend with him."

"I'm sure the two of you will get along fine and have fun." She prayed she was doing the right thing.

"Marsha," her father said. "If Ryan doesn't feel comfortable with William yet, then—"

"He'll never feel comfortable if he doesn't get to know his father. And he can't get to know *Will* unless he spends time with him," she said.

"Why do I have to stay the whole weekend?" Ryan asked. "Can't I go for the day then come home?"

"No." She glared at her father over the rim of her coffee mug, daring him to interfere.

"But Grandpa and I haven't finished our chess game."

"The chess game can wait," Marsha said.

Ryan swung his pleading gaze to his grandfather. "Tell Mom I don't have to go, Grandpa."

Marsha and her father locked gazes.

"Listen to your mother, Ryan." Her father got up from his chair and walked out of the room.

"This sucks," Ryan muttered then winced. "Sorry, Grandma. I meant to say this stinks." He shoved a spoonful of cereal into his mouth then mumbled, "I'm not going to have any fun."

"I know," Marsha said.

"Then why are you making me go?"

She could hardly admit she hoped to appease her own guilt. "Because." If she let him, her son would go round and round in circles with her for hours.

"What does it matter if I get to know him better? We live in California and he lives here."

Will had made the same point yesterday—like father like son. How did she think the two males would form a bond if they saw each other every few years? She'd made the decision to bring Ryan and Will together and she had to give them every possible opportunity to be father and son even if that meant returning to Stage-coach each summer for a week or two no matter how busy their schedules became. And if they ran into a conflict, then she'd invite Will to California.

"C'mon, Mom. Next week I'll do something with Will," Ryan said.

Marsha refused to give in to Ryan. She carried her cup and bowl to the sink. "Pack enough clothes for two days and take the sleeping bag Grandma has in the closet and your bed pillow." She paused in the kitchen doorway. "And don't take your e-reader with you."

Ryan's groan echoed in her ear as she retreated down the hallway.

## Chapter Nine

"What are you and Ryan going to do?" Conway asked.

"I have no idea." Will stood next to his brother Friday evening staring out the barn doors as they watched Ryan and the twins play tic-tac-toe in the dirt by the porch.

"He doesn't look happy," Conway said.

That was the truth. Ryan hadn't smiled once since he'd driven off with Will after working at the church. "Got any plans with the twins tomorrow?" Maybe Will and Ryan could tag along.

"Isi wants me to paint over the water stains on the ceiling in the upstairs hallway." Conway grinned. "Want to help?"

"No, thanks." The last thing Will cared to do with his day off was home repairs. "I thought about taking Ryan to the junior rodeo in Growler, but he doesn't like rodeo." He wished his son felt differently about the sport. He would have loved teaching him how to rope a steer.

"You'll think of something to do."

Will checked his watch. Eight o'clock. Bedtime was at least three hours away. He cut across the yard and stopped in front of the group.

"We're bored." Javier pointed a dirty finger at his cousin. "Ryan's bored, too."

"Ryan's mom wouldn't let him bring his e-reader, so he can't read us any stories," Miguel said.

Now he understood why Ryan wouldn't make eye contact when they'd waited for their burgers at Vern's Drive-In—the teen blamed Will for having to leave his favorite hobby at home. "What do you say we head to the swimming hole?"

The twins popped up and shouted, "Yeah!"

When Ryan remained silent, Javier said, "You wanna swim with us? There's a board we can jump off."

"It's called a pier, dummy," Miguel said.

"Do you know how to swim, Ryan?" Will asked.

"Yeah, but I didn't pack my trunks."

"I've got an extra pair you can use," Will said.

When Ryan remained silent, Javier tugged his arm. "Uncle Porter taught me how to do a cannonball. Can you do one?"

Ryan nodded.

"Mig and Javi, go change into your swim shorts and don't forget towels." The twins raced into the house.

"I'll find those trunks for you." Will walked off, hoping they'd swim for at least a couple of hours, then maybe Ryan would be tired enough to go to bed and Will wouldn't have to worry about entertaining him.

Forget a long swim—in less than an hour Will and Ryan were back in the bunkhouse, twiddling their thumbs. "Is there a TV show you like to watch on Friday nights?" Will pointed the remote at the big screen mounted to the wall across from the beds.

"I don't watch a lot of TV. I mostly read."

Determined to find a program they'd both enjoy,

Will flipped through the channels then stopped when he came across a documentary on the Hoover Dam. Maybe Ryan would be interested in the science behind the construction of the dam. "You like popcorn? I've got the microwavable kind in the cupboard."

"Sure." Ryan stretched out on Johnny's old bed and listened to the TV.

Will handed Ryan a bag of popcorn, then sat on his bed. "Do you know how much cement they used to build the dam?"

Ryan shook his head.

"Over four million cubic yards."

"How much water does it store?" Ryan asked.

"Almost 9.2 trillion gallons from the Colorado River."

"How long did it take to build?"

"Five years." Will suspected the kid was testing him.

"How much did it cost?"

"Almost forty-nine million."

Ryan gaped at Will. "How come you know so much about the Hoover Dam?"

Not from reading about it—that was for sure. "I watch a lot of how-things-are-made shows." He drank from his water bottle.

"Did you have to go to a special school to learn how to build houses?"

Will was excited that Ryan appeared interested in what he did for a living. "I learned by doing it." He compensated for his reading disability by observing others in action and then going off on his own and building things from memory.

"I like to do science experiments," Ryan said. He reached into his duffel bag and pulled out a notebook.

"I keep my ideas in a journal." He handed the pad to Will. "You can take a look, if you want to."

"What kind of experiments are these?" Will perused the sketches in the notebook, impressed with their complexity.

"I describe them in the margin." He pointed to the handwriting along the edge of the page.

Will's eyes strained to make out the letters, but his brain couldn't put them in the right order. "This looks interesting," he said. The drawing contained a series of overlapping circles and lines.

"One day I want to experiment with solar panels to see if I can use them to create rain."

"The ranchers in the southwest would appreciate that," Will said.

"I explain how the panels work here." Ryan flipped the page. "Since you know about construction, maybe you could tell me if my idea will work."

Sweat broke out across Will's brow. "You know who'd be a better judge?"

"Who?"

"Your uncle Conway. He could give you advice based on his experience managing a crop with little annual rainfall."

"Yeah, sure." Ryan shut the notebook.

Will hated that he'd put a damper on his son's excitement, but he hadn't been able to make sense of all the scientific notes Ryan had scrawled in the journal. "Is there someplace you'd like to go tomorrow?"

"Have you ever been to the Yuma Territorial Prison?" Ryan asked.

"You want to tour a prison?"

"I heard there's a library in the prison and that some

of the prisoners were taught music, Spanish and German."

Will had lived his entire life in Stagecoach and had never toured the state park where the prison was located. "Sure. We can drive out there tomorrow."

"Cool." Ryan tossed his popcorn bag in the trash. "I think I'm gonna go to bed now."

"I've got a couple of things to do before I turn in," Will said. He left the bunkhouse and walked out behind the barn where he stared at the stars. Would there ever come a day when he could let his guard down with his son?

THIRTY MINUTES BEFORE the Sunday-morning service Marsha's mother called down the hallway. "Will's here with Ryan."

"I'll be right there." Marsha checked her image in the mirror then added a swipe of pink lip gloss before walking outside.

"Good morning." She stopped next to Will's Ford and glanced between the two males—neither looked any worse for wear. "You've got ten minutes to change clothes, Ryan."

"Okay." Her son hefted his duffel onto his shoulder and hugged the sleeping bag to his chest. "Thanks for taking me to the prison. See you tomorrow."

"Sure thing."

After their son walked off, Marsha said, "You guys toured a prison?"

"Ryan said he'd always wanted to see the old Yuma Territorial Prison." Will's expression sobered. "He wasn't happy that you made him leave his e-reader behind."

"I hope he didn't take it out on you."

"He survived, but I'm sure he'll want to catch up on his reading today."

"What did Ryan mean about seeing you tomorrow?" she asked.

"I said I'd take him to that fancy model shop on Main Street in Yuma to pick out a model that we can build together."

"Do you plan to put it together at the farm?"

"If it's all right with you. And you can drop Ryan off at the farm whenever he wants to work on it."

"Is he staying the night with you tomorrow?"

"If he wants, otherwise I'll drive him home later."

"That's fine." She motioned to the cars pulling into the church lot. "Would you like to attend the service with us? The parishioners are excited about the new classroom wing. I'm sure they'd love to talk with you about it."

"No, thanks." He opened the truck door.

"Before you go…" She gathered her courage. "I wanted to cash in on that rain check for our missed lunch earlier this week."

"What did you have in mind?"

"Maybe a picnic supper."

"The three of us?" he asked.

"No. You and me."

"I don't mind if Ryan wants to tag along."

Why was Will suddenly backing away from her? "Picnics aren't really Ryan's thing. How about Tuesday evening?"

"Sure." He hopped into the driver's seat and shut the door before the word *goodbye* escaped Marsha's mouth.

After he drove off, she made her way to the church, ignoring the funny feeling in her stomach.

Will acted as if his day with Ryan had gone well, so why did she sense he wasn't telling the whole truth?

"Which one do you want?" Ryan stared at the selection of models.

When Will had suggested they build a model together during the drive home from the prison, Ryan had jumped at the opportunity. He studied the boxes in Ryan's hands. A small boat and a single-engine prop airplane. "I was hoping to put together a more complicated model," Will said.

"You were?"

He pointed to the top shelf. "Maybe a coast guard ship, or that rocket looks pretty cool."

"The rocket's three feet long," Ryan said.

"The table in the bunkhouse is six feet long. We could build an aircraft carrier." He moved his finger down the shelf. "This one is five feet long."

"If we get a big one, I won't be able to take it to California with me," Ryan said.

"You don't have to wait until next summer to see it again. You're welcome to stay at the farm for Thanksgiving or Christmas break." The idea of his son leaving in a couple of months bothered Will now that they were becoming comfortable with each other.

"I kind of like the rocket ship." Ryan glanced at Will then looked away. "But it's got lots of parts and looks difficult."

Did Ryan assume Will wouldn't be able to put it together? "I worked on models when I was your age and I think we can handle this one."

"You built models?" Ryan asked.

"Yep. I've always liked working with my hands."

"It's expensive, but Mom gave me spending money for the summer and I can help pay for it."

"No way," Will said. "I've got fourteen birthday presents to make up to you."

Ryan smiled—the first genuine smile he'd offered Will.

Will reached for the rocket ship from the top shelf. What was two hundred dollars anyway? He spent that in one weekend at a rodeo—if he included the entry fee, gas and food.

"After you turn sixteen, if you spend the summer in Stagecoach, your uncle Buck will help you work on a car."

"What do you mean?" Ryan trailed Will to the checkout.

"You'll need a car in high school, won't you?"

"Maybe."

"We'll buy an old beater and fix it up. Buck's a whiz at cars and Conway and I are pretty good with engines, too. Between all of us we'll make sure you have a nice set of wheels."

"Awesome."

Will hoped he hadn't overstepped his bounds in promising Ryan a car for his sixteenth birthday, but he wanted to give his son a reason to return to Stagecoach.

Back at the farm Ryan organized the rocket parts into piles for each section of the model. He read the directions out loud and Will listened while he mentally matched up the pieces with the image on the box.

"Which part should we do first?" Ryan asked. The teen wanted to build the model in a well-planned, organized way, whereas Will would have put pieces together at random.

"You choose where you want to start," Will said.

Ryan's eyes lit up when he realized Will had given him the green light to spearhead the project. He mapped out a game plan and when he'd finished explaining the details, it was already nine o'clock.

"You're welcome to sleep here tonight if you want to work on the rocket," Will said.

Ryan stared longingly at the table strewn with parts. "I better get home before my grandpa goes to bed."

"If your mom will drive you over here, you can work on the rocket whenever you want." Will hoped Ryan wouldn't take him up on his offer, because he wanted them to do this project together.

"Do you think the twins will mess with this?" Ryan asked.

"I'll make sure the boys understand this is grown-up stuff and they shouldn't touch it."

Will talked about the models he'd built in the past with his friends and before he knew it, they'd arrived at the pastor's house.

"Thanks again for buying the model."

"See you later." Will watched Ryan enter the house and for the first time since he'd met his son, he felt they were making a connection.

*What about you and Marsha?*

Tomorrow night he'd find out if they were meant to connect, too.

"I THOUGHT YOU were in bed?" Marsha stepped onto the patio at eleven-thirty Monday night and found Ryan reading. After Will had dropped him off a short while ago, he'd rambled on about the rocket Will had bought. Marsha's father hadn't appreciated hearing that his grandson and Will had discovered a hobby they could enjoy together and had gone to bed early.

"Reading in the dark is bad for your eyes." She stretched out in the lounge chair.

Ryan ignored her comment and used his finger to turn the page on the gadget's illuminated screen.

"We haven't talked much lately. Tell me more about the tour you and Will took of the Yuma prison," she said.

Ryan set the e-reader aside. "Mom?"

"What?"

"Will can't read."

Marsha's heart skipped a beat. "What makes you say that?"

"I showed him my science-experiment journal and asked him to read the data I'd collected and he got this funny look on his face."

"That's hardly proof Will can't read."

"When we were at the prison, I pretended I couldn't see one of the signs on the wall and I asked him what it said. He stumbled through the words, then turned all red and walked off."

Marsha wished Will had confided in Ryan about his learning disability. It wasn't her news to tell.

"And when we were putting the model parts together, he never read the directions. He looked at the picture of the rocket on the box, then guessed which parts went together."

"Maybe he wanted to work on the easy sections first?" she said.

Ryan shook his head. "I've been researching stuff

on reading problems and I think I know what's wrong with Will."

"Oh?"

"He's got dyslexia."

*Wow.* Her son never ceased to amaze her. "How can you tell?"

"He skipped over some words and read really slow, dragging out the pronunciation of the letters." Ryan sat forward in the chair. "And people with dyslexia have messy handwriting like Will's. He paid for us to get into the prison with a credit card and after he signed the slip, the lady asked him to show her his license, because she couldn't read his signature."

"Honey, that doesn't prove—"

Ryan left the chair and paced across the patio. "I can help him, Mom. I can teach Will how to read."

She'd never seen her son this animated, but obviously he felt strongly about wanting to help his father.

"Do you know that Will watches a lot of TV and memorizes stuff he hears?"

"What do you mean?"

"We saw a program on building the Hoover Dam and I asked a bunch of questions about it and Will knew the answers, because he'd seen a show on the dam. Then he said that he learns things by watching people do them first."

Ryan was talking so fast, Marsha had trouble making sense of everything.

"Because he can't read well, Will memorizes what he hears and sees."

"Amazing." She didn't know whether she meant Will or Ryan's excitement over his father's learning disability.

"Do you know what this means, Mom?"

"I'm afraid I don't."

"If Will learns how to read, he could be smarter than both of us." Ryan spread his arms wide. "He could build a space station one day."

"Honey, Will seems happy building houses and fixing churches." Then again she'd never asked him if he loved his job.

"But if Will could read better, he could learn all kinds of really important stuff."

"I wouldn't tell your grandfather that you don't consider the addition of classrooms to his church important stuff."

Ryan didn't crack a smile. "Do you think Will would let me tutor him?"

"I don't know."

"Should I ask him?"

That Ryan appeared eager to get together with Will again was a positive sign. Still, she felt compelled to warn Will what Ryan had up his sleeve, and she hoped it wouldn't blow up in her son's face.

"THIS IS SO PRETTY," Marsha said. She had no idea the natural spring nestled next to a rocky incline existed south of Stagecoach. "Whose property are we on?"

"It's government land." Will placed folding chairs on the ground at the edge of the spring.

Marsha opened the cooler she'd brought and removed a bowl of fried chicken and a bottle of red wine.

"You thought of everything," he said, eyeing the wine and plastic cups.

Once they were seated and had helped themselves to the chicken Marsha's mother had made, she asked,

"How's the construction on the classroom wing coming along?"

"Ben's waiting on a delivery of insulation. After that's installed, we'll put up the wallboard, patch the seams and paint." He sipped the wine. "This is good."

"I wasn't sure you drank wine."

He winked. "A girl I once dated educated me on fine wines."

A burning sensation filled Marsha's chest. She didn't care to hear about the women in Will's past, but she would like to know how she stacked up against them. "May I ask you a personal question?"

"Sure."

"Have you ever been in love?"

"Serious love?"

She laughed. "Is there any other kind than serious?"

"I thought I was in love once." He took another sip of wine. "I proposed to her."

*You wanted to know.* Marsha toyed with the piece of chicken on her plate. "Who was she?"

"Her name was Rachel. We met at a rodeo."

"What happened?"

"I had a dream the night after I'd proposed to her." Will's stare bored into Marsha. "I dreamed about you."

Her heart stuttered. "Me?"

"You were crying and telling me how sorry you were."

Tears burned her eyes.

"After the dream, I couldn't stop thinking about you or the day I'd told you to get an abortion." He shrugged. "I broke off my engagement to Rachel and I haven't seen her or heard from her since." Will's eyes darkened.

"For months afterward I wondered about you. Where you were. How you were doing."

"But you never asked my parents about me."

"Shoot, no." Will chuckled. "Your father scares the bejesus out of me."

"I kept in contact with Hillary Bancroft," Marsha said. "When we talked on the phone, I'd find a way to ask if she knew what you were doing, who you were dating or if you'd married. She never mentioned that you'd gotten engaged."

"No one knew." He grinned. "I'm surprised you kept tabs on me."

"Why would you be surprised? You're Ryan's father."

"I've never understood why you wanted to go to the prom with me in the first place. When Buck told me to ask you out, I thought he was nuts."

"Really?"

"You were a pastor's daughter and I was Will Cash." He helped himself to a second piece of chicken. "Why would a churchgoing good girl want to be seen with a guy like me?"

"Because I was a *good girl* didn't mean I was immune to your bad-boy charm. I thought you were the most exciting guy in our class."

"I should have known not to get carried away with the pastor's daughter," he said.

"I got carried away, too, Will."

"I was more experienced, I should have had better control."

"I'll take that as a compliment." After their laughter faded, she said, "We made an amazing child together."

"I won't argue with you there. Ryan showed me his

notebook of ideas and it blew me away." Will topped off her cup with more wine. "He's a bright kid."

She wasn't sure now was the right time to bring up Will's dyslexia, but he opened the door when he mentioned the journal. "Ryan's pretty impressed with your knowledge, too."

"Impressed how?" Will set aside his plate and wiped his mouth and fingers with a napkin.

"He says you're a walking encyclopedia of knowledge on the Hoover Dam."

"He told you I had trouble reading at the prison, didn't he?"

"He mentioned that." She searched for the right words then gave up. "Ryan wants to teach you to read."

Will bolted from his chair and walked to the water's edge. "They tried to help me in school, but the reading exercises never clicked and my grandparents couldn't afford to pay for a private tutor."

"You don't have to accept Ryan's offer. I just wanted you to know in case he brings up the subject with you."

"How did he figure out I was dyslexic?"

"He noticed a few things you did and researched them on the internet."

"It's always going to be there between you and me and Ryan, isn't it?"

"What are you talking about?" she asked.

"Both of you are smart and I'm not."

"Wait a minute. I've never discussed your IQ with Ryan. I don't know what grades you got in school."

"Ds and Cs." He scowled. "But you've thought about me not going to college, haven't you?"

"I—" She wouldn't lie to him. "Yes." She'd wondered if things between them would have ended differently if Will had gone to college, too. Would he have settled down sooner and offered to marry her, if she'd told him that she'd kept their baby?

"Actually," she said, "Ryan believes if you were a better reader, you'd be smarter than him."

"He said that?"

She nodded.

"I'll talk to Ryan about my dyslexia, but right now I owe you a long overdue apology."

"For what?"

"I should have apologized when you first arrived at the farm, but I was too angry and confused after learning about Ryan."

"No, Will. I'm the one who needs to say I'm sorry."

"Do you regret not being truthful with me from the beginning?"

"Yes. No matter how valid I believed my reasons, you had a right to know I didn't go through with the abortion."

"I'm sorry for taking advantage of you the night of the prom," Will said.

She forced a smile. "Are you sorry because you wished you'd had sex with that cheerleader?"

"Truth?"

The setting sun framed Will in a seductive glow and it drew her out of her chair. "Yes," she said, walking toward him. "Tell me the truth."

"Once I got a glimpse of what was under your dress, I forgot all about Linda Snyder."

Marsha stopped in front of Will—close enough to touch him. She threaded her fingers through his. "You were a bad boy with the most soulful brown eyes. Every day you rode into the school parking lot on that old Harley, my heart raced."

He squeezed her hand.

"Look at you now. When guys in our class are losing their hair and growing potbellies, you're as *hot* as ever."

His fingers brushed her cheek. "Tell me to stop."

"No." She flung her arms around his neck and pressed herself against him.

He groaned. "This is a mistake."

"We've made one before, and we both survived." If the past had taught Marsha any lessons, it was that she worried too much about the future.

## Chapter Ten

Will had dreamed of holding Marsha in his arms and loving her—not like a groping teenager but an experienced man who knew how to please a woman.

His mouth hovered over hers, drawing out the anticipation. Her blue eyes softened—did she want him as badly as he wanted her?

He pressed his mouth to hers and thoughts of taking it slow dissipated when her tongue teased his lip. It would be like this between them—hot and raw as the rocky desert beneath their feet. He swept his tongue inside her mouth and tasted a hint of wine then deepened the kiss, making sure there was no doubt in her mind that he wanted her. Right here. Right now.

He lowered the strap of her sundress, moving the material aside, then nuzzled her bare skin. He worked the buttons of her bodice free and stared at her naked breasts. She was stunning. When he strummed his thumb over her pink nipple, she moaned. Their gazes locked as she ran fingers through his hair, coaxing his head lower. He found her boldness incredibly sexy.

Their passion escalated and when she lifted her leg against his thigh he felt his control slip. "I don't want us to make love in a pickup again." They should have a mattress beneath them so he could sink into her body and kiss every inch of her silky skin.

He shivered, unable to focus when she nibbled his jaw. They were adults, not teens. Marsha deserved better than a quickie with a cowboy in his pickup. His ego demanded he show her that he was a skillful lover and not a sex-craved bad boy who could hardly keep it together more than a few minutes.

*If you had your own place you could take her there.*

Will ignored the voice in his head. The last thing he needed when he made love to Marsha was a reminder that he lived in a bunkhouse with his brothers.

"Let's get a motel room," he said.

"I don't want to wait that long." She pressed her hands against Will's chest until he backed up a step, then she slipped out of her panties and tossed the scrap of lace on the ground.

She stood before him, breasts exposed and no panties on beneath her sundress. He wasn't a saint and when her fingers reached for his belt buckle he closed his eyes and gave up the noble fight. He'd make love to her anywhere she wanted—backseat, truck bed or against the tailgate.

Her hand slid beneath the waistband of his BVDs, and she pressed her nails into his naked backside. "Touch me," she whispered.

"You're making me crazy." He buried his face between her breasts and inhaled her feminine scent. Inch by inch his fingers worked the hem of her dress higher. He caressed her thigh then moved to her bare bottom and squeezed a moan from her. She lifted her leg, resting her knee against his hip, then shuddered when he stroked her heat.

Marsha was too damned hot and he'd nixed his plan

to finesse his way through their lovemaking after she'd removed her panties. "Get my wallet from my pocket." Marsha turning up pregnant after they'd had sex once had scared the bejesus out of him. From that day forward he'd never been caught unprepared. She handed him the wallet and he removed a condom.

"Let me." She rolled the condom on, and he gritted his teeth, hoping he wouldn't embarrass them both and lose control. As soon as she finished, he shoved her skirt higher and buried himself inside her.

For a moment they froze—barely breathing as they stared into each other's eyes. A hint of a smile tugged the corners of her mouth and he kissed her, hoping to convey what he felt in his heart. No matter what happened between them after tonight, he'd never regret this moment with her.

Tonight he could pretend that he was the kind of man Marsha envisioned herself growing old with. The kind of father she wanted for their son. The kind of son-in-law her parents would approve of.

He was none of those things, but in Marsha's arms, he almost believed he was perfect.

As soon as Marsha opened the door off the garage and turned on the light she swallowed a gasp. Her father sat at the kitchen table in his pajamas and robe. And he didn't look happy.

"What are you doing up this late?" It was one-thirty in the morning and her father usually conked out in his recliner before the late-night news ended.

"Your dress is dirty." His gaze raked over her.

"I'm a grown woman, Dad."

"You're still my daughter and you're the mother of

my grandson. I expect you to behave appropriately and not—" his gaze zeroed in on the dirt smudges along the hem of her dress "—come home looking like a girl who spent the night with a man she has no business being with."

"Stop right there before you say something you'll regret."

A standoff ensued. Marsha gave in first, hating that her father was ruining a special night for her. Because of his health, she pushed aside her irritation and removed two mugs from the cupboard and filled them with water. Then she added an herbal tea bag to each and placed them in the microwave. When the timer dinged, she brought the mugs to the table and sat.

"I've always had feelings for Will, Dad." She ignored his scowl. "I don't know where things will lead between us, but life is too short not to take chances."

"You have a son." Her father pointed to the hall-way leading to the bedrooms. "Ryan's your number one priority."

"I've made Ryan a priority all these years." She blew on her tea. "That's why I've never married or invested my energy in personal relationships."

"I don't see how a relationship with William Cash will have a positive impact on my grandson."

Marsha realized that she and her father had never had it out after he'd learned Will had fathered Ryan. Maybe it was time. "What is it exactly that you don't like about Will aside from the fact that his mother had children fathered by different men?"

"Aimee Cash was no good," he said.

"You can't hold Will's mother against him. He had no control over her actions." Good grief, had her father forgotten the home she'd been born into before he'd adopted her? "Will's grandparents were highly respected in the community."

"Ely and Ada should have taken their daughter to church every Sunday instead of allowing her to come home pregnant over and over again."

"Going to church doesn't make you a Christian, Dad, and it doesn't make you worthy or better than others."

"I don't want to see Ryan get hurt," he said.

She suspected her father's worry over Ryan was compounded by his cancer diagnosis and concern that one day he wouldn't be there for his grandson. "I respect and love you, Dad. You and Mom took me into your home and hearts and raised me as your daughter." She squeezed his hand. "It wasn't easy living up to your expectations. I know I disappointed you deeply when I gave birth out of wedlock." She considered her words carefully. "I wanted to shield you from as much gossip and criticism as I could. That's why I've stayed in California."

Her father's already pale face grew whiter. "I never insisted that you stay away from Stagecoach."

"I know, but it bothered you that I was a single mother and it hurt me that when I brought Ryan home you'd always suggest I attend the second church service on Sunday mornings. I knew it was because fewer people attended that service. And you rarely went anywhere in public with me, but you'd always take Ryan on errands with you."

He stared into his mug.

She hadn't said those things to hurt her father, but he had to understand that his decisions impacted her, too. No one was perfect. And since they were having a heart-to-heart, she might as well put everything on the table. "I told you who Ryan's father is this summer, because I selfishly want your forgiveness before it's too late." Her eyes watered, but she refused to cry.

"I should be the one begging your forgiveness." His smile was tinged with sadness. "You were a gift from God to your mother and me and I'll always be grateful that you're my daughter."

Marsha's heart swelled to twice its size. "I don't know what's going to happen between me, Will and Ryan, but I hope you'll give us your blessing while we try to find our way together."

Not a week went by since Ryan had been born that she hadn't thought of Will. Dreamed of him at night or asked Hillary what he was up to. Marsha's crush on Will hadn't dissipated through the years and she needed to deal with her feelings for him so she could move forward with her life—with him or without him.

"Forgiving you for keeping William a secret is easy, Marsha."

She sensed a *but* coming.

Her father pressed his lips into a thin line while he considered his words. "*But* I can't support you pursuing a personal relationship with him."

"Why not?"

"You forget that I'm not only a pastor but I'm also a father, and I believe my daughter deserves better than William Cash."

"What do you mean better?"

"You two aren't compatible in the broadest sense."

"Good grief, Dad, we grew up in the same town. Went to the same high school."

"You've got a Ph.D. and William hasn't gone to a

trade school never mind college." He grunted. "How will you carry on a meaningful conversation with him if all he knows how to do is hammer boards together?"

Shocked by her father's bluntness, she hoped his declining health wasn't stealing his compassion for others. "I've never heard you speak that way before."

"You wanted honesty and I'm giving it to you." He smacked his palm against the table. "I want better for my daughter and grandson."

"What if Will makes me happy? What if Will and Ryan form a bond?" No way was she telling her father that Ryan was excited about helping Will overcome his reading disability.

"You're meant for better things than being stuck in a small town with a husband who works sporadically on construction jobs. Are you willing to throw away your career for a man who'll never reach your level of success? Think about what kind of example that sets for Ryan?"

"You don't need to worry about Ryan. He'll blaze his own path regardless of where he lives or who's in his life."

"Not with a Cash cowboy as his father," he protested.

"For a man who isn't supposed to judge others you sure have a lot of opinions about Will."

"William won't encourage Ryan to go to college. He'll tell my grandson there's nothing wrong with using his hands to make a living."

There was nothing wrong with a blue-collar job if the person enjoyed what they did and made a decent living at it. Marsha couldn't shake the feeling that there was more behind her father wanting the best for her and

Ryan. What drove him to say these insensitive things about Will was anybody's guess.

"What's going to happen to your mother after I die?" he said.

"What do you mean?"

"The church will continue on, but your mother and I have used up most of our savings fighting my cancer."

Was money the reason her father decided not to continue treatment for his disease?

"I've got a fifty-thousand-dollar insurance policy on myself. Your mother can't live off of that for long." He spread his arms wide. "This house belongs to the church. She'll be forced to move out after I'm gone."

"I'll take care of Mom," Marsha reassured him. "She's welcome to live with me and Ryan wherever we are."

"She never worked a day since we married. How will she find employment? She'll need to pay for her own health insurance."

"Don't worry, Dad. Mom won't have to fend for herself."

"That's why it's important that you push Ryan to succeed in school and college. He may need to take care of you one day."

"You know," she said. "You tell your parishioners to have faith when things go wrong in their lives. You tell them that God has a plan for everyone and they should trust Him. You need to listen to your own advice."

"As a pastor I believe those things but as a father I fear if you and William end up together, he'll squander the money you earn. What if he quits working for Ben Wallace and expects you to support him?"

"Why would he do that?"

"Aimee Cash is his mother. She lived off of other men and when she got pregnant, they ran out on her. Then she showed up at the farm, had her baby and left the child with Ely and Ada when she ran off again."

"Will's not like his mother. He's not a user."

"You haven't been with him long enough to know that."

The conversation was going downhill. "You've made it clear where you stand with me dating Will. I'd appreciate it if you wouldn't share your feelings with Ryan." She took her cup to the sink.

"Marsha."

Heart aching, she faced her father. Her need to clear her conscience had brought her a sense of peace, but it had brought her father more worry. This was not how she wanted him to spend his last months on earth—anxious about the future of his wife, daughter and grandson. "What, Dad?"

"Never mind."

She retreated to her room and sat on the bed, rocking as silent tears ran down her face. Tonight she'd held out hope that maybe there was a path to happily-ever-after for her, Will and Ryan—a dream she'd held close since she'd given birth to her son. Why couldn't her father see that Will *was* the right man for her?

She'd be a horrible daughter if she didn't try to make her father's last days on earth worry-free but did that mean she had to sacrifice her own happiness?

"LATE NIGHT?" WILL MOTIONED to the coffeepot when Porter walked into the bunkhouse at the crack of dawn Wednesday morning.

"No, thanks. I'm going to shower then catch a nap," Porter said.

"I thought you broke up with that Betsy chick?"

"She's been history for a while. I hung out with Stacy last night."

"Is that what you call sleeping with a woman—hanging out?"

"We didn't have sex. We went to a movie and then talked until—"

"The sun rose." Will chuckled.

"You're usually not this chipper before you go to work," Porter said.

"Maybe because last night I was with Marsha…talking."

Porter hooted. "Are you two making up for lost time?"

Will wouldn't say last night made up for fourteen years, but it was a heck of a start.

"Where do things stand between you guys?" Porter asked.

Will wasn't ready to divulge any personal facts about his and Marsha's relationship. "We're taking things slow."

"Does this mean you've forgiven her for keeping Ryan a secret?"

"It does." Will had been hurt that Marsha hadn't been truthful with him from the beginning, but in all honesty, he'd been living with his own guilt for years and had felt only relief that she'd gone against his wishes and kept their baby.

"You've been out of the game for a while, so if you need any dating advice, I'm your go-to man." Porter headed to the bathroom.

Will set his mug aside, grabbed his cowboy hat and keys then left the bunkhouse. The sun had cleared the horizon and already the temperature was climbing. Ben had called earlier, informing Will that he'd be late to work and for Will to go ahead and begin framing the classroom walls.

Thoughts of making love to Marsha filled Will's head during the drive to the church. Now that they'd been intimate and the experience had been over-the-top amazing, Will was confident that he, Marsha and Ryan would become the family they should have been from the beginning.

After he parked in front of the church, he glanced at Pastor Bugler's house. He smiled when he envisioned Marsha asleep in bed, her long blond hair mussed and a dreamy expression on her face.

He took that image with him into the church and surveyed the work he and Ben had done, but his thoughts wandered to Marsha. He admired her beauty, intelligence and independent streak though most men might find those qualities intimidating. He was in awe of her successful career and ability to raise a child by herself. She was an amazing woman and he was nowhere near good enough for her.

Yet when their clothes had come off and it was flesh against naked flesh, they'd been more than compatible. Except for Ryan, he and Marsha might not have a lot in common, but other couples had begun with less and made a go of marriage. Will would be lying to himself if he didn't admit that he eagerly anticipated his next date with Marsha.

The sound of a throat clearing made him jump inside his skin. He spun and came face-to-face with Pastor Bugler. He appeared pale and his shoulders slumped forward as if it took too much effort to stand straight.

"'Morning, Pastor."

"William."

Will was in too good a mood to allow the man to goad him.

"Ben and I are putting up the framework to separate the classrooms today." When the pastor didn't comment, Will took a folding chair and placed it next to him. "Have a seat."

After he sat down, Will asked, "What's on your mind?"

"I want you to leave my daughter alone."

Will stared, at a loss for words.

"I know what you did with Marsha last night." Color flooded the old man's wrinkled cheeks, making his face appear feverish.

Feeling like a teenager being taken to task, Will said, "Your daughter and I are adults. What we do is none of your business."

"I'm her father and a father's duty is to protect his child. You wouldn't care about that, because you were never there for Ryan."

Will forced himself to speak calmly. "Your daughter didn't give me an opportunity to be there for Ryan." As he spoke the words, he knew Marsha's father was right. No matter what he'd liked to think, he'd been wild and young back then and he wouldn't have been there for his son even if he'd known about him.

"Marsha should never have told you about Ryan." The pastor's hand shook when he rubbed his brow.

Will was torn between defending himself and worrying about the old man's health. "I know you don't approve of me or my family, but that doesn't change the fact that I fathered your grandson and I have a right to be involved in his life."

"He doesn't need a man with little education. A man who doesn't attend church. A man whose mother was wild and—"

Will sliced his hand through the air. Everything the pastor said was true, but it didn't mean that Will had to listen to it. "I get that you don't believe I'm good enough for your daughter, but Marsha's and Ryan's opinions of me are the only ones I care about."

"I helped raise my grandson. Ryan is a decent young man with a bright future. He needs to be with people like him and his mother—educated, intelligent and ambitious. You'll drag them down."

"Then it was all an act?" Will said.

"What are you talking about?"

"The day you came to the farm and socialized with my family. Pretending to get along with my brothers and spending time with my nephews?"

"I have no quarrels with your brothers and their families."

"Only me."

"Yes. As I said before—"

"I heard. I'm not good enough for your daughter or grandson." Anger sizzled in Will's gut.

The sound of a vehicle pulling into the church lot echoed through the construction site. Ben had arrived.

The pastor pointed a finger at Will. "I will go to my grave fighting to keep you away from Marsha and Ryan." He stood then shuffled off, leaving Will feeling more insecure than ever before.

The hours passed slowly as they framed the classrooms. If his boss sensed Will's bad mood, he held his tongue. Will contemplated bringing up the pastor's visit with Marsha, but what if he was right—Will wasn't the best man for her and Ryan? How could he continue seeing Marsha when he knew how badly it would upset an ailing man during his last days on earth?

When the workday ended, Will packed up his tools. He needed to put together a plan, but before he drove off, Marsha came out of the house and waved. He watched her hurry toward him, feeling that familiar ache in his chest that exploded each time he saw her.

"Will." Her smile hurt his heart.

Today she wore her hair pinned to her head in a messy bun and he longed to remove the clip and run his fingers through the gold strands.

"Did my father talk to you today?"

"He did."

"I was hoping I'd have a chance to prepare you first." She stared into the distance for a moment then shook her head. "He's upset that we…"

"I got that impression," he said.

"Please don't take this wrong or think last night wasn't special, because it was." She rubbed her forehead as if their conversation was giving her a headache. "Because of my father's health, I don't want to upset him further."

Will's heart skidded to a halt. "What are you saying?"

"I think we need to cool things off between us."

"Meaning…?"

"We probably shouldn't go on any more dates."

She might as well have punched him in the throat—he'd rather feel physical pain than the excruciating ache ripping his chest apart. Stupidly he'd hoped Marsha would defy her father and insist on being with Will. "Do I have to keep my distance from Ryan, too?"

"Of course not. I want you guys to do things together."

So this was it—another one-night stand with Marsha and they were finished. He hopped into his truck and shut the door. At least this time he knew for sure that he hadn't gotten her pregnant.

He drove off, refusing to look in the rearview mirror, fearing if he saw Marsha's face, he'd stop and beg her to take him back—the pastor be damned.

As he sped down the highway, Will's thoughts drifted to Buck. He'd treated his brother like crap, forcing him to leave town and for what?

Will had lost the girl again before he'd ever really had her.

## Chapter Eleven

"Mom, can I come in?"

"Perfect timing, Ryan." Marsha's Friday-morning tutoring session had ended and the students were logging out of the chat room. "What's up?"

"I found a book that gives tips on how to help dyslexic people. Can I buy it?" He sat in the chair across from her desk. "It's half price on Amazon."

The past week her son had researched dyslexia more than he'd read on his e-reader or played chess with his grandfather. Marsha wished she'd had the courage to stand up to her father and continue seeing Will, but she'd gone to bed the night after they'd argued in the kitchen and she'd lain awake until dawn. Her father had been the reason she'd achieved her goals. If not for him and her mother adopting her and providing her with a loving, nurturing childhood, who knows what would have become of her. In the end, she'd decided that she'd sacrifice her dream to be with Will if it set her father's mind at ease during his last months on earth.

She was proud of Ryan for wanting to help his father, but wasn't sure how receptive Will would be after she'd cooled things off between them several days ago.

"I know what Will's problem is. When he read that

sign in the prison, his eyes kind of jerked back and forth. The jerkiness is called tracking. There are a bunch of exercises Will can do to force his eyes not to move so much when he reads."

Her heart ached at the excitement in Ryan's voice, but if he spent too much time with Will, her father would get upset. Marsha didn't want anything to come between grandfather and grandson, but she also didn't want to interfere with Ryan and Will developing a relationship.

"Can I go to the farm with Will after he quits for the day?"

*Will.* Marsha walked across the room and stood in front of the window facing the church. After she'd shut Will out, she'd resorted to spying—right now he and Ben were installing windows. "Where's Grandpa?"

"Grandma drove him into Yuma to that old folks' home," Ryan said.

A handful of her father's church members were residents of an assisted-living facility. Since they were no longer able to attend Sunday services, her father ate lunch with them on Fridays, then read scripture. With her parents out of the house, Marsha didn't have to worry about her father seeing Will and Ryan together.

*What about when he discovers Ryan took off with Will?*

"So can I go to the farm or not?" Ryan asked.

She opened her mouth to say *not,* but stopped short. She'd made the decision to spend the summer in Stagecoach in order for Will and Ryan to become better acquainted. As much as she yearned to be an obedient daughter, she refused to sacrifice her son's relationship with Will to please her father.

"It's all right with me if you go, but ask Will first. He might have plans."

"Okay." Ryan bolted from the office.

Marsha returned to the desk and made notes on the students she'd tutored, wishing all the while she could go to the farm with Ryan, too.

"Look who came out here to check on our progress," Ben said.

"Hey, Ryan." Will forced a smile.

"Hi, Will. Hi, Ben." Ryan nodded to the power tool in Will's hand. "Are you almost done putting in the windows?"

"We will be after this one."

Ben's phone went off and he said, "Excuse me a minute."

"What have you been up to?" Ryan hadn't been out to the farm to work on the model rocket in a while and each night when Will walked into the bunkhouse and saw the parts strewn across the table, he was reminded again of Pastor Bugler's warning to keep his distance from his grandson and daughter.

"I've been doing some research," Ryan said.

Will's gut clenched. He knew what was coming— Marsha had warned him. "Research on what?"

"Dyslexia."

"Oh?" The urge to flee dug its claws into Will, but he forced himself to make eye contact with his son.

"Remember when you had trouble reading the sign in the prison?"

No father wanted to appear weak in front of his child, but he reluctantly admired Ryan's courage for bringing up the subject. "Yes."

"I saw your eyes move a lot."

"I have trouble focusing when I read." No sense acting as if his problem wasn't a big deal.

"We can fix it." Ryan smiled.

*We?* The heavy feeling in Will's chest lightened.

"The condition is called tracking," Ryan said.

"You sure it can be fixed?"

"There's lots of stuff you can do to keep your eyes calm when you read. I can help you, Dad. If you'll let me."

*Dad.*

Will's throat tightened—Ryan had called him *Dad* for the first time. He'd done nothing to earn the title, yet his son was offering him a chance to fill the role. Swallowing hard, he glanced toward his boss, who was still talking on his phone. "How can you help me?"

"You need to exercise your core." Ryan pointed to Will's stomach. "Do sit-ups and stuff."

"My eyes are in my head, not my stomach." Will grinned.

"Good posture helps you sit still and focus better when you read."

"What else should I be doing?"

"Use a ruler or piece of paper to cover up all the words in a sentence, except the one you're reading. It makes your brain slow down and your eyes won't jump as much."

"That sounds logical."

"When you get good at keeping your eyes steady, you're supposed to read out loud, 'cause if you hear your voice, it forces your brain and eyes to work together better." Ryan pointed to himself. "You could read one of my books on my e-reader and I'll listen to you."

Ryan's intentions were heartfelt and Will didn't want to dampen his excitement. Shoving aside his embarrassment, he said, "When do you want to show me these exercises?"

"I can go to the farm with you after you're done working."

"As soon as Ben and I put this window in, I'll be ready."

"I'll get my Kindle." Ryan took off and a minute later Ben ended his call and they finished installing the window.

"The plumbing fixtures arrive on Monday," Ben said as he gathered his tools.

"You want me to pick them up at the store in Yuma?" Will asked.

"I'll get them. We'll meet here a little after ten Monday morning."

"Sounds good. Enjoy your weekend." Will started the engine, then turned on the air conditioner to cool the cab. Ryan came out of the house with Marsha. She was a sight for sore eyes in a pair of cutoff jean shorts, a blue tank top and her blond hair blowing in the breeze. All he had to do was look at her and his testosterone level shot through the roof.

"Hi, Will."

"Hello, Marsha."

"You're sure Ryan staying at the farm won't interfere with your weekend plans?"

She had trouble making eye contact with him. Maybe she wasn't as confident about cooling things off between them as she claimed to be. "I don't have any plans," he said.

"See you later, Mom." Ryan hopped into the passenger seat and shut the door.

"I'm sorry, Will. I hope you're not upset about Ryan wanting to help with your dyslexia."

"It's nice to know he cares about me." He cleared his throat. "When should I have him home?"

"Whenever you get tired of him."

"You know how to reach me."

Marsha nodded. "Have fun."

"Is something wrong with my mom?" Ryan asked as Will drove off.

"I don't know. Why?"

"I think she's sad."

"Maybe she has a lot on her mind." Will didn't care if Marsha's decision to end their relationship before it had gotten off the ground upset her. She'd made the call—she had to live with the consequences. "You hungry?"

"Sure. I can always eat." Ryan smiled. "Ask my mom. She goes to the grocery store a lot."

Will chuckled. His grandmother had complained about her six grandsons eating the family out of house and home. After a pit stop at Vern's Drive-In and two chicken-finger baskets with fries later, they arrived at the farm. Conway and Porter's trucks were missing and the twins weren't playing in the yard. "Looks like everyone's gone," he said.

"Bandit's here." The dog lay sprawled in the dirt next to his doghouse.

"How would you like to teach me the reading techniques down by the fishing pond and we'll take Bandit with us?"

"Do I have to fish?"

"Nope." But Will needed a way to calm his nerves

and fishing relaxed him. "You get Bandit and I'll grab my gear in the barn and pack a cooler of drinks."

Fifteen minutes later, Ryan and Will set down the cooler, fishing gear and two lawn chairs beneath the pecan tree by the water hole. Bandit rolled in the dirt a few feet away.

"What kind of fish are in the pond?" Ryan asked.

"A few carp and one or two catfish."

"That's all?"

Will chuckled. "The water gets too hot during the summer to support a larger population so the few that are in there are strong enough to survive." Will baited his hook.

"What smells?" Ryan pinched his nose and grimaced.

"Stink bait."

"Gross."

"I'm going to aim for the far corner of the pond." Will cast his line, but it fell short of his goal and he reeled it in.

"Can I try?" Ryan asked.

Will handed over the pole.

Ryan's motion was awkward and the line barely made it to the center of the pond. "It's harder than it looks," he said.

"Try again."

The hook landed at the water's edge. He expected Ryan to give up, but he kept at it. Will's chest filled with pride. On the fifth try, the line sailed across the pond and splashed in the far corner.

"That was perfect," Will said.

Ryan grinned and handed the pole to Will who balanced it against the chair before he opened the cooler and passed Ryan a can of soda then popped open the tab on a can for himself.

"How long does it take before they bite?" Ryan asked.

"Could be five minutes or two hours."

"You want to start the exercises to help your eyes stay steady?"

"I've had this problem all my life. It might not be as easy to fix as the research claims."

"That's okay. If it takes forever, I don't mind helping you."

Humbled, Will said, "Show me what to do."

Ryan scooted his chair closer and turned on his e-reader. After enlarging the print of an article entitled "Tracking and Dyslexia," he pulled a piece of paper out of his pocket, folded it into a neat square, then covered all the words, except the first word in the first sentence.

"You have to read each word out loud so your eyes don't wander," Ryan said. "Once you read the word, move the paper to the next one and read it."

Will forced himself to relax. "These." He moved the paper, but his eyes flickered to the word he'd already read. Increasing his focus only made the letters in the second word shuffle places. The word looked familiar… "Exercise."

"Exercises," Ryan said. "It's plural."

"Exercises." Will focused harder. "Have. Im…pro… ved. Eye. T…rack…ing."

"That's good," Ryan said.

Will appreciated his son's enthusiasm, but he felt the beginnings of a headache building behind his eyes. "Ability."

"You read the whole sentence." Ryan's smile faded. "What's wrong?"

Forcing his brow muscles to relax, Will said, "When I concentrate, I get a headache."

"Okay, we can do a different exercise." Ryan took the e-reader from Will and turned it off. "We'll strengthen your core."

"All I have to do is a few sit-ups and I'll read better?"

Ryan shook his head. "More than a few sit-ups."

Shoot. Will would rather do physical exercise any day than fumble through words. "Are you doing sit-ups with me?"

"Sure." Ryan sank to the ground then laid flat on his stomach. "You gotta lift one arm and then the opposite leg up and hold it for 5 seconds, then do the other arm and leg. Watch."

After the demonstration Will joined Ryan in the dirt and counted the seconds. After repeating the exercise for each arm and leg, Ryan said, "It's a lot harder than it looks on the YouTube video."

"Tell you what. I'll practice these before I go to bed every night and after a week I'll let you know if I notice a difference when I read."

"Maybe you could write down your reps in a log book."

"That's a good idea." The kid wanted proof that Will would keep his word.

"And maybe you should read two pages a day. One in the morning and one at night until you don't get a headache anymore."

Ryan truly wanted Will to succeed. How could he not follow through with the exercises and written log, even if it didn't help him read better? "Hey, Ryan, can I ask you a question?"

"Yeah, sure."

"Did I ever cross your mind through the years?"

Ryan rubbed Bandit's belly.

"It's okay if you don't want to answer," Will said.

"I kind of tried not to think about you." Ryan's blue gaze connected with Will's for a moment before he glanced away.

"I don't know if your mom told you, but my father wasn't around when I was growing up."

"He wasn't?" The curiosity in Ryan's voice gave Will the courage to open up.

"My dad never married my mother. It really bothered me as a kid and I bugged my mom with a lot of questions about him. Where was he? Why didn't he want to see me?"

"Mom said if I ever wanted to know about you, she'd tell me, but she always looked kind of scared when she said that. I thought I wasn't supposed to ask." He shrugged. "After a while I got used to it being me and Mom and I kind of forgot about you."

Ryan's honesty hurt, but Will pushed it aside. "I wasn't that close with my mother," he said. "If I had been, I might not have wanted to know more about my dad."

"Did you get to meet your dad?"

"I did."

"What did he say?"

"Not a whole lot. He was married and had two little kids younger than me."

"Did he want to be your dad?"

"No."

"Were you angry with him?" Ryan asked.

"Yes." Will gathered his thoughts. "I want you to know…"

"What?"

"That you don't have to do things with me, if you don't want to."

Ryan frowned. "You don't want to do stuff together?"

"Yes, I want to do things with you, but I'm probably not the kind of man you envisioned for a father."

"You mean because you have dyslexia and didn't go to college?"

*Ouch.* "Yeah." It was more painful to have this conversation with his son than it had been to face his own father years ago.

"It's not your fault that reading is hard. And you're trying to learn."

Living up to Ryan's standards wouldn't be easy, but Will was going to give it his best effort.

"Can I ask you a question?" Ryan said.

"Sure."

"Are you disappointed that you got a son who doesn't like rodeo?"

Will would be a liar if he didn't admit that when they'd first met, he'd wished Ryan was more like him. But after getting to know his son and realizing the depth of his intellect, Will acknowledged it was his own insecurities that had made him worry the two of them would have nothing in common.

"I like you the way you are, Ryan. I couldn't be more proud of your academic accomplishments, and I know you'll go on and do great things in whatever career you choose."

"It's okay with you then if I want to get good grades and go to a really good college?"

Will squeezed Ryan's shoulder. "It's more than okay."

"Can I ask a personal question?" Ryan said.

"Sure."

"Did you love my mom when…you know…" Ryan looked away.

"I was a wild teenager in those days, and I only thought about myself. Your mom was a smart girl with a bright future ahead of her and I should have known better not to take advantage of her. For that I'll always be sorry."

"Do you like my mom now?"

"I've always liked your mother and admired her." That was the truth. The fact that the memory of his prom date with Marsha had been responsible for breaking off his engagement to Rachel proved Marsha meant more to him than he'd realized.

"I'm glad 'cause I really want you guys to get along and for us to do stuff together."

Easier said than done after Marsha had decided to keep her distance.

"Did you know my grandpa is dying?" Ryan said.

The abrupt change of subject startled Will. Marsha must have had a talk with Ryan about his grandfather's cancer.

"I heard," Will said.

"My mom doesn't know that my grandpa told me a couple of days ago when she and Grandma went to the store."

"I'm sorry about your grandfather, Ryan. I know he's very special to you."

"How close were you to your grandfather?" Ryan asked.

"My grandfather was like a father."

"My grandpa said he's not afraid of dying, because he knows he'll meet God when he gets to Heaven."

Will had gone to church on a few occasions in the past, but he was no expert on religion or faith. Maybe that was one reason the pastor remained adamant that Will keep his distance from Ryan. "I'm glad you're close to your grandfather."

It was the truth, but Will didn't want to wait until Marsha's father took a turn for the worse before he and Ryan didn't have to sneak around to be together. The trick was convincing the pastor that there was room for both of them in Ryan's life.

"Look, Dad! You got a bite!" Ryan scrambled off the ground and lunged for the pole then reeled the fish in.

"That's a catfish," Will said.

"It's huge. What do I do with him?"

"Do you want to eat him or toss him back?"

"I like fish but..." Ryan shook his head. "We'll let him live, so the twins can catch him."

Will held the flopping fish steady and wiggled the hook out of its mouth. "You want to toss him into the pond?"

Grimacing, Ryan held the fish, then released him at the edge of the pond.

"For a first-time fisherman you've got real potential." Will's chest swelled with affection for his son. Too bad Ryan's grandfather saw so little potential in Will.

## Chapter Twelve

"What are you going to do?" Hillary slid a comb through Marsha's damp hair.

"I'm not sure." Marsha had stopped at the Bee Luv Lee Hair Salon for advice from her friend, but in the end it had cost her the price of a haircut.

"I know." Hillary pinned a section of hair to the top of Marsha's head then snipped a quarter inch off the ends.

"Don't keep me in suspense."

"Stand up to your father for once."

Marsha winced. There'd been numerous Saturday nights in high school when her father had nixed Marsha's plans with Hillary, because he'd been overprotective. "I held my ground with him." *Sort of.*

"Just because you're not interfering in Ryan and Will's relationship doesn't mean you stood up for yourself."

"It's more complicated than that." Marsha might as well tell the truth since it was only the two of them in the beauty shop. "Will and I…"

Hillary gasped. "Had sex?"

Marsha nodded.

A dreamy expression settled over Hillary's face. "It

sounds so romantic…reuniting with your first love. Was it better the second time around?"

*Oh, yeah.* "The sex was great. Perfect."

"Then what happened?"

"I went home and my father guessed what I'd done…" She fisted her hands beneath the cape, then winced when her nails bit into her palms. "He believes I can do better than Will."

"Don't tell me you listened to him," Hillary said.

"How can I go against his wishes when he's dying?"

"What did Will say when you told him about all this?"

"I didn't tell him. I said I thought it was better if we kept our distance from each other."

"That was cruel."

"It would have been worse if we'd kept dating. My father would have become more upset and the last thing I want is for him to confront Will."

Hillary sectioned off more hair and snipped the edges. "You're crazy if you believe Will is going to wait until your father dies and then take you back with open arms."

Marsha knew the risks when she'd pushed Will away, but in the farthest reaches of her heart, a secret dream had taken hold after she'd given birth to Ryan—one day she'd reunite with Will and they'd become a family.

*And now you've made a mess of things with Will.*

"I love Will." Admitting her feelings out loud lifted a huge weight off her chest.

Hillary set the scissors aside. "Can I be blunt?"

"Of course."

"Are you attracted to Will because he's different from you?"

"What do you mean?"

"I thought you and Will were all wrong for each other in high school. You two are polar opposites."

"We're not that different." Marsha wanted to believe so anyway.

"You make twice as much money as Will does," Hillary said. "And you went to college. You live in California and Will has never moved from the place he was born."

"Money and education aren't the only things that make people compatible or incompatible."

"Maybe, but money and education influence how a person views the world and their place in it," Hillary said.

"It's possible that Will and I look at some things differently but as long as our values match up, I don't see a problem." As brave as her words sounded, Marsha worried Will might not feel her equal.

Hillary fluffed Marsha's hair. "If things don't work out for you and Will, at least he and Ryan are getting along."

And no matter what happened between her and Will, Marsha pledged to do everything possible for father and son to remain close.

"How's your dad feeling lately?" Marsha asked.

"Tired. I can tell his body is slowing down." Hillary sorted through her brushes then grabbed the hair dryer. "Is he in a lot of pain?"

"Not that I can tell."

"I don't want to be nosey or rude but how long does he have now that he quit the cancer treatments?"

"The doctor told my mother anywhere from six

months to a year and a half. Staying involved in the church is giving him the strength to keep going."

Hillary laughed.

"What's so funny?"

"I don't think it's his Sunday sermons that are lighting his fire, rather the fact that he found out Will is Ryan's father."

Could it be true? Had Marsha's father caught a second wind when he learned the truth about his grandson's father? Was his determination to keep Will away from Marsha and Ryan the source of his renewed energy?

Hillary flipped on the blow-dryer and spent the next fifteen minutes styling Marsha's hair. When she finished, she said, "You look like you're in your early twenties."

"I can thank my parents for that. They were adamant I wear sunscreen before I went outside every day."

"It paid off. You've got beautiful skin." Hillary stuck her arm in front of Marsha's face. "Look, I'm covered in freckles and scaly red patches."

After paying for her trim, Marsha hugged Hillary. "Thanks for being such a good listener."

"All part of the job, honey."

If only Hillary could do more than listen and fix Marsha's aching heart.

"HEY, WILL," BEN SAID, Friday morning at the church. "Take tomorrow off."

Seven days had passed after Ryan had spent the weekend at the farm. Every night since then Will had practiced his reading exercises and had written his progress in a journal. His *homework* had kept his mind off how much he missed Marsha. "I thought we were installing the plumbing."

"I'm driving up to Phoenix to see the home and building expo at West World. You're welcome to ride along, but I thought you'd rather stay in town and be with Ryan." Ben removed his tool belt. "How's the rocket coming along?"

"We're about a third of the way done." Ryan had coaxed Will into staying up until two in the morning to work on the model after they'd returned from the fishing pond. They'd finally called it quits when Porter had come home from one of his hot dates.

Will packed his tools away. "Do you want to work on Sunday after the church service lets out?"

"We're a week ahead of schedule. Monday's soon enough."

Will and Ben spent the next hour cleaning the area before they quit for the day. Will waited for Ryan to come outside and talk to him, but he never showed so Will drove off. When he reached the highway he headed to the Triple D Ranch. He needed advice and he trusted only one of his brothers to give it to him straight— Johnny. He'd rather vent to Johnny than sit at the farm on a Friday night and think about Marsha and Ryan.

When he parked in front of the foreman's cabin, he noticed Johnny's vehicle next to the barn. A bale of hay flew out of the hayloft window and Will hollered at his brother. "Johnny!"

"C'mon up."

Will entered the barn and climbed the ladder to the loft. His brother sat on a bale, guzzling from a water bottle. "Hotter 'n hell today," Johnny said.

Will sat down across from Johnny. "How's Addy doing?"

"She turned a month old yesterday." Johnny finished his water. "She's colicky, but I discovered how to get her to stop crying."

"Oh, yeah?"

"You can't tell a soul." Johnny lowered his voice. "I put Addy on the mechanical bull."

"No way."

Johnny grinned. "You should see her eyes when the thing starts up—as big as an owl's."

"No kidding."

"She likes the swaying motion." Johnny's expression sobered. "Scares me to death to think about it, Will, but I'm almost certain Addy's going to follow in her mother's footsteps and become a roughstock rider."

"Hey, there's nothing wrong with adding a few strong women to our family tree." Marsha would make a great addition to the Cash clan.

"How are things between you and Ryan?" Johnny asked.

"Good. We went fishing at the pond last weekend." He wasn't ready to tell his brothers yet that his son was tutoring him in reading.

"Catch anything?"

"The old catfish that's been living in the muck for the past two years," Will said.

"You two didn't eat him, did you?"

"No."

"Good. Conway wants to keep him in there, because he's the only fish the twins ever catch."

Enough beating around the bush. "Johnny, I need your advice."

"I'm listening."

"Pastor Bugler warned me to keep my distance from Marsha and Ryan."

"Why would he do that?"

Will appreciated his brother's outrage, but they weren't in elementary school anymore and Johnny didn't have to fight off the bullies for Will.

Johnny grimaced. "Pastor Bugler said you weren't good enough for his daughter and Ryan, because you're a Cash."

"Mom tossed us all under the bus when she got pregnant by every Tom, Dick and Harry in Arizona."

"What did Marsha say about all this?"

"I didn't tell her about her father's talk with me."

"She's not trying to keep you from seeing Ryan, is she?"

"No one's going to stop me from being with my son." Will removed his cowboy hat.

"Okay, if Ryan's not the problem then…" Johnny's mouth widened into a grin. "It's Marsha, isn't it?"

Will nodded. "It's complicated."

"How so?"

"We went out on a date a couple of weeks ago and… things got out of hand."

Johnny quirked an eyebrow. "How out of hand?"

When Will glanced away, Johnny chuckled. "Was it good?"

"Knock it off. No one got in your grill when you started sleeping with Shannon."

"Okay, you had sex with Marsha and that part was all good. Then what happened?"

"She said it wasn't the right time for us to be together."

"What are you going to do?" Johnny asked

"What else can I do, but honor her wishes and keep my distance?"

Johnny shook his head. "Do you think her father got to her, too?"

"I don't know."

"Did you ask her?"

No, he hadn't. But what if Marsha and her father had gotten into a fight over him? How could he hold it against her if she'd gone along with the pastor's wishes? He stood. "I better go."

"So you're giving in and letting her old man call the shots in your relationship?"

"What am I'm supposed to do, Johnny?" He stormed to the other end of the loft. "I can't come between Marsha and her father—the man's dying of cancer."

"Hey, I'm not a cold heartless bastard. I'm sure it's tough on Marsha and Ryan knowing they're going to lose their father and grandfather, but it's not their job to convince the pastor that you're good enough for them."

"What are you talking about?"

"You have to change Pastor Bugler's mind about you."

"If I piss the old man off he might turn Ryan against me."

"So you're going to sacrifice your own happiness with Marsha and Ryan because deep down you don't really believe you're good enough for them, do you?" Johnny said.

The blood drained from Will's face. Was he taking the easy way out because he didn't believe he deserved to be Marsha's husband or Ryan's father? Was he making excuses for himself and accepting the pastor's interference rather than trying to prove he deserved a second chance with the two people who'd come to mean the most to him?

"I don't know where to begin to win over Pastor Bugler," Will said.

"You could start by going to church."

He gaped at Johnny. "That's the last place Marsha's father wants to see me."

"Are you sure? He's a man of God, Will. Maybe he needs a little reassurance that your heart is in the right place before he believes your intentions toward his daughter and Ryan are sincere."

Johnny made it sound simple—as if attending a church service was all it would take to win the old man over. A relationship with God wouldn't erase who his mother was or what she'd done. And God couldn't make his birth father claim him as his son or fix Will's dyslexia and send him to college.

"Church is about faith," Johnny said. "Give Pastor Bugler a reason to have faith in you."

"I'll think about it."

"Let's get out of this oven." Johnny descended the ladder first, then said, "Shannon wants to baptize Addy and Dixie wants Nate baptized, too."

"What church?" Will asked.

"Don't know. Maybe I'll mention Pastor Bugler to Shannon and see what she thinks." Johnny slapped Will's shoulder. "Wouldn't hurt to have family sitting in the pews with you."

"Say hi to Shannon." During the drive to the farm, Will mulled over his brother's advice. When he pulled up to the bunkhouse, he'd made a decision. Johnny was right—like he was most of the time—Will had to give

Pastor Bugler a reason to believe he was the best man for his daughter and grandson.

He'd go to church Sunday.

"LOOK, MOM." RYAN POINTED behind their pew Sunday morning.

Marsha peeked over her shoulder and thanked God she was already sitting down. What in the world was Will doing in her father's church?

"Can he sit with us?" Ryan asked.

How could she say no? "Sure."

Ryan left the pew and a moment later appeared with Will by his side.

"Hello, Marsha." He flashed his bad-boy smile.

"Good morning, Will." Aware of the churchgoers staring at them, she scooted over, thinking Ryan would sit next to her, but Will claimed the seat. The scent of his cologne spawned a mental vision of Will sliding his hand up her naked thigh and she fanned her face with the program. *Good grief.* She had no business thinking about sex in God's house.

"Hey, Dad," Ryan said, loud enough to draw attention to them. "What are you doing after church?"

"How would you like to go for a trail ride out at the Black Jack Mountain Dude Ranch?" Will asked.

"I've never ridden a horse." Ryan peeked around Will and spoke to Marsha. "You want to go, Mom?"

Marsha didn't immediately answer—she was still wincing after Ryan had called Will *Dad* out loud. She wasn't sure how many people her parents had told about Will; she suspected not many. She had a feeling the pastor's daughter and Willie Nelson Cash would be the topic of conversation at the parishioners' dinner tables later today. "We'll talk about it after the service, Ryan."

The organist began playing and the choir—with her mother in the lead—walked through a side door and took their places behind the pulpit. After they lined up, Marsha's mother made eye contact with her and smiled. When her gaze shifted to Will, she stopped singing, but recovered quickly and looked at Marsha with shocked eyes. Toward the end of the hymn, her father entered the sanctuary and gave the signal for the parishioners to stand then recited the opening prayer.

Following the prayer, her father read a list of church announcements. Then the choir sang again. As was his custom, her father glanced through the pews, making eye contact with all the churchgoers. When he got to Marsha's pew and noticed Will, his mouth pressed into a thin line and he visibly struggled to control his reaction. Marsha felt horrible that both her parents had been caught off guard today.

"Many of you have been asking when the new classroom wing will be ready for the children. Today, one of the men responsible for the construction project has joined us." Her father nodded to Will. "Perhaps William Cash would be willing to offer an update on the progress?"

Will tensed and Marsha thought he might refuse, but then he stood. He nodded to the folks seated near them. "Barring any unforeseen circumstances, the new wing should be ready soon. We're waiting on the flooring for the bathrooms, then we'll paint the walls and install the carpet." Will sat down.

"Thank you, William." Her father delivered his sermon—
so far the longest twenty minutes of Marsha's morning.

Once the lecture ended, the choir sang two hymns
as the donation plates were passed through the pews.
When the plate arrived at Will's side, he added a twenty-
dollar bill—her father couldn't find fault with Will's
generosity. She added ten dollars, then passed the plate
on.

After the collection, Marsha's father recited the final
prayer before walking to the front doors. The parishioners filed out of the pews, beginning at the front of
the church. After the first six rows emptied, Marsha
clutched Will's arm. "Let's wait for the church to clear
out."

"Are we going riding this afternoon?" Ryan asked.

She glanced at Will. "Sure, you can go." Her father
slept all afternoon after Sunday services.

"Are you coming, Mom?" Ryan asked.

She hadn't been officially invited. "I think your father wants to spend the day with you."

"I'd like for all of us to go," Will said.

Marsha's heart skipped a beat, though she told herself that Will was being nice to her because Ryan was
present. She doubted he'd have invited her otherwise.

"Thank you, but—"

"Do you have other plans?" Will asked.

"No."

"Have you ever been to Black Jack Mountain?"

"No," she said. But that's as far as the conversation
got before her father approached them. And he wasn't
smiling.

"What a surprise seeing you in one of my pews,
William."

"Pastor Bugler." Will stood and offered his hand. "I enjoyed the sermon."

"Grandpa, we're going to a dude ranch. You want to come along?"

"You're more than welcome to join us," Will said.

"No, thank you." Marsha's father spoke to her. "I thought you were helping your mother cook the Sunday meal? Aren't we having guests tonight?"

Every Sunday her father invited a family from the church to share supper with him and Marsha's mother. "I helped Mom with the potato salad this morning. All you have to do is put the hamburgers on the grill."

Her father's mouth turned down but he didn't challenge her. "When will you be home?"

"I don't know." She wasn't sure what had gotten into her, but if Will had had the courage to attend church, then she could show some spine and not let her father intimidate her.

"We'll probably catch a bite to eat afterward," Will said.

"Be careful." Her father stared Will in the eye. "Neither Ryan or Marsha knows how to ride a horse. See that they don't get hurt."

"I will, sir."

Once her father exited the church, Marsha swore she heard the air from Will's lungs escape in a loud rush. "Give us fifteen minutes to change clothes," she said.

Will waited beneath the shade of a paloverde tree. He prayed he'd made the right decision in asking Marsha to join him and Ryan for a horseback ride. After talking with Johnny, he didn't want to believe that what he and Marsha had shared meant so little to her.

*What if you're wrong? What if she doesn't love you?*

*Then I move on.*

Which wouldn't be easy when he looked into his son's blue eyes and saw Marsha.

## Chapter Thirteen

"How long has Mack worked at the dude ranch?" Marsha asked when Will turned off the main highway onto the road leading to the property.

"A little over a year." Will glanced in the rearview mirror—Ryan remained occupied with his e-reader. As soon as they'd gotten into the truck, the teen had turned on the device after telling Will he'd downloaded a book detailing the history of the Arizona dude ranch. The out-of-the-way guest ranch was located sixty miles south of the pecan farm along the Mexican border.

"Mack knows a lot more about the history of the place," Will said.

"It was once a mission outpost for Jesuit priests over 300 years ago," Ryan said. "This book says there's a famous adobe building that they use as a dance hall for the ranch guests."

"I'm looking forward to a tour," Marsha said.

For a woman who'd suggested they cool things off between them, Marsha didn't appear uncomfortable in his presence. Too bad Will wasn't as calm—his gut was twisted in knots. He shifted in his seat, hoping his plan today would go off without a hitch. He pointed out the windshield when they reached the guest parking area. "That's the dance hall."

Ryan put his e-reader away. "How long is the ride?"

"I'm not sure." Will didn't want to reveal the arrangement he'd worked out with Mack until after they'd parked and met up with his brother. They walked toward the cast-iron bell guests were allowed to ring when Mack emerged from the barn.

"Been waiting for you three." Mack shook hands with Will, passing him a key in the exchange. "Nice to see you, Marsha." He switched his attention to his nephew. "Ryan, wait until you see the horse I picked out for you to ride."

"I've never ridden before," Ryan said.

"That's why I chose Warrior. He's a pro in the desert."

Ryan cracked a smile. "Warrior doesn't sound like the name of a gentle horse."

"He's the best we've got. The snakes don't scare him." Mack glanced between Will and Marsha. "C'mon, Ryan. I'll show you the horses, they're all named after rodeo clowns."

When Marsha stepped forward, Will caught her hand. "I've got different plans for us while Ryan's out riding."

Marsha smiled. "What are you up to, Will Cash?"

"When I spoke to Mack about the possibility of bringing you two today, he mentioned that a family vacationing here has a thirteen-year-old daughter, who loves to read as much as Ryan does. Her parents haven't been able to entice her out of their guest cabin all week."

"Mack's doing a little matchmaking," she said.

"He thought the kids might enjoy each other's company."

"What's the girl's name?"

"Amanda Stevens. Her father's an international businessman and her mother's a concert pianist." Will grinned. "Amanda wants to be an astronaut."

Marsha laughed. "They should hit it off then."

"Mack thought so. That means you and I have time to ourselves."

"To do what?" She struggled to keep a straight face.

"You'll see." Will took Marsha's hand, the muscles in his shoulders relaxing when she didn't resist his touch. So far, so good. He took the path that wound through the property and ended in front of a cabin nestled against a rocky incline.

"What are we doing here?"

*Keep it cool and casual.* He slid his hand into his pants pocket and his fingertips touched the ring nestled in the cotton lining. "We have the use of the cabin while Ryan's on the trail." Ignoring Marsha's wide-eyed gaze, he slid the key into the lock and opened the door.

Marsha entered first, then stopped in the middle of the room and twirled in a slow circle. "It's lovely."

Will shut the door and flipped the lock, then allowed himself to look his fill at Marsha—the beautiful woman who was once the young girl he'd taken to the prom. She was a real-life fantasy—*his fantasy*—and the men in California were idiots for allowing her to remain single.

This afternoon Will hoped to change that.

"I'm not sure this is a wise place for us to have a talk." Her gaze swung to the bed.

"I don't want things to end the way they did between us."

"I'm sorry if I hurt your feelings. I—"

"Wait." He closed the distance between them and gently tugged a strand of hair. "Did you enjoy my kisses?"

Her gaze softened. "Of course."

He'd known that, but he wanted to hear her admit it out loud. He brushed his mouth over hers in a slow caress. "Did you like the way I touched you?"

Her body shivered. "Yes."

"And you agree that we're compatible in bed?"

She clasped his face between her hands and rose on tiptoe, initiating the next kiss. "Maybe you could save whatever's on your mind until later." She nibbled on his chin.

*Oh, man.* He hadn't thought his plan through very well when he'd decided to bring Marsha to the cabin to propose.

Her mouth skimmed his throat and he decided *marry me* could wait until after they made love. He swung Marsha into his arms and carried her to the bed, then set her on her feet and tossed aside the cowboy quilt.

Their gazes locked, she unbuttoned her blouse, revealing a red lace bra. His mouth went dry. "Do your panties match that bra?"

"Yes." She placed his hands against her belt buckle and Will needed no further urging. In a matter of seconds her belt was on the floor and he was shoving her jeans over her hips. She fell against the mattress, giggling as he tugged off her boots and socks. Wearing nothing but sexy red lace, she crooked her finger. "Your turn."

Once she had him naked, he spent the next five minutes exploring her silky skin with his mouth and hands.

When her lace bra and panties landed on his pile of clothes, he asked, "Are you sure?"

"I'm always sure with you."

Will had dreamed of making love to Marsha slowly, caressing every square inch of her body and learning her sweet spots. He buried his face against her neck, inhaling her scent—perfume and sweet, sexy Marsha. When he lowered his mouth to her breasts, her breathing grew faster and she reached between their bodies, caressing him with an urgency she'd never shown before.

Marsha pressed Will onto his back and crawled over him. With a sassy smile she rolled a condom on him then took him inside her—so much for his plan to go slow. They shot off like a couple of bottle rockets toward the heavens.

A short while later, the sound of birds chirping penetrated Will's consciousness and Marsha snuggled closer to his side, sliding her thigh between his legs.

"Mmm…that was nice," she whispered.

"I didn't mean for this to happen when I brought you into the cabin," he said.

Marsha toyed with his nipple. "We're both adults. We can have sex if we want."

Will wanted it to be more than sex. He leaned across Marsha's body and scooped his jeans off the floor, then rummaged through his pocket and removed the ring.

"Marsha," he said. "Our relationship back in high school didn't get off to a great start."

"It didn't get off to any start."

"I let you down when I told you to get an abortion, but I hope you've forgiven me for that."

"There's nothing to forgive, Will. You were as young and scared as I was."

"And had you told me you hadn't aborted Ryan, I would have helped you financially," he said.

"I'm sorry, too. I never should have kept our son a secret from you."

"I want to let go of the past and start over. I want the three of us—you, me and Ryan—to be a family."

"In a sense we're already a family," she said.

"Then let's make it legal. I want to be your husband, and I want you to be my wife and together we'll be Ryan's parents."

"What are you saying?"

He opened his fingers to reveal the diamond solitaire resting on his palm. "Marry me."

Instead of happy tears, she clutched the sheet to her breasts and sat up in bed. Not the reaction he'd hoped for. "I don't know what to say."

"Say *yes*." His heart thudded painfully—could she hear the muscle pounding through his chest wall?

"I realize this is happening fast, but we've already lost fourteen years as a family and I don't want to play it safe. Take a leap of faith with me, Marsha."

Her eyes swung between the ring in Will's hand and his face. "What's the matter?" he asked.

"The timing…. It's…all wrong."

"Forget about the timing. I love you, Marsha. I think I fell in love with you the night we went to the prom." He reached for the ring finger, intending to slide the diamond on, but she curled her fingers into her palm. Shocked, he stared at her fist.

"My father's battling cancer and—"

"I'm going to prove to your father that I'm worthy of you. I promise. I won't let you down."

"His health is a major concern right now. I don't want to upset him," she said.

Will opened his mouth to protest, but she cut him off. "You can't understand how badly I disappointed him when I became pregnant out of wedlock."

"Then wouldn't he be relieved we're making our relationship legal?"

"It's not that simple," she said. "He doesn't believe you're good enough for me or Ryan."

So her father had gotten to her, too. Now he knew the reason she'd pulled away from him. "Your father's looked down his nose at the Cash family for years. So what? He'll get over his prejudice when he sees I'm a good husband and father."

"The emotional drama may be too much for him right now. I want to make his last days stress free."

Although he sympathized with the tightrope Marsha walked with her father, Will sensed she wasn't being completely truthful with him. "There's more to you wanting to put our relationship on hold than pleasing your father, isn't there?"

The starkness in her gaze sent a jolt of panic through Will. "There's no sense denying we're compatible in bed and we'll always be connected because of Ryan, but you can't deny we've gone different ways since graduation."

"We were going different ways before we graduated high school, Marsha. What does that have to do with the three of us becoming a family?" She didn't answer him. "Does my lack of education bother you?"

Her silence shot through his heart like a bullet.

"You may know more about chemistry and scientific formulas, but we share the same beliefs about the things that really matter." He smiled. "You saw how important family is to me when you spent the day at the farm."

"Yes, but—" her gaze skirted his face "—Dad brought up a good point. I've been working hard in hopes of obtaining a teaching position at a major university and—"

"I'd never interfere with your career plans. I get how important teaching is to you," he said.

"That's easy to say now, but will you be as supportive after you see the long hours I work? Between teaching and tutoring and Ryan's after-school clubs we're hardly home."

"C'mon, Marsha. Have I given you any reason to believe I'm the kind of man who needs a woman's undivided attention 24/7?" He didn't give her a chance to answer. "When two people love each other, they find a way to carve out time to be together. I'm not concerned about that."

"Ryan and I live in California. Your roots run deep in Stagecoach and you've never been apart from your siblings."

He hated that this conversation was stressing her out. He leaned in and kissed her, trying to calm her fears. "As much as I love my brothers and sister, you and Ryan are my family now."

"What about my mother? After Dad's gone, she'll need someone to take care of her. She's never worked outside the church and because of Dad's medical expenses, their retirement savings have shrunk and she might need financial help down the road."

"Your mother is always welcome to live with us."

"I won't have money for a down payment on a new home until I pay off my student loans."

Will frowned. "I don't expect you to support me. I'll work construction jobs in California like I do here."

"But it may take a while for you to find one."

Will wasn't sure what to say. She was offering excuse after excuse—had he misjudged her feelings for him? With a queasy stomach, he got out of bed and took his clothes into the bathroom to dress. When he came out ten minutes later, Marsha was still in bed. It took all his strength not to strip down again and remind her how good they were together.

"You know what?" he said. "I think you're hiding behind your father's illness, because you're not sure how you feel about me." When his statement didn't provoke a response from her, he said, "Do you love me, Marsha?"

She opened her mouth to speak but no words came out.

Her silence might as well have been a fist to the gut because the air in his lungs froze, and his chest threatened to crack wide open. He'd gotten it all wrong. Feeling like an ass because Marsha didn't love him enough to put their relationship first, he stuffed his feet into his boots, all the while praying she'd try to stop him from walking out of the cabin.

No such luck.

His bruised and battered ego felt like it had gone twelve rounds with a heavyweight champion.

"I'll be waiting for Ryan in the cantina." He shut the door quietly, resisting the urge to slam it hard enough to break the hinges.

How the heck had a surprise marriage proposal turned into the nail that sealed his coffin?

"HEY, DAD!" RYAN RACED toward Will, Mack right behind him.

Will smiled at the excitement in his son's voice. No

matter what happened between him and Marsha, he'd always be grateful to her for giving him the gift of his son.

Ryan skidded to a stop. "I made a friend. Her name's Amanda and she's going to be an astronaut one day."

"That's impressive. Sounds like you enjoyed horseback riding."

"It was okay," Ryan said.

Will caught Mack's eye roll.

"Amanda's friending me on Facebook and we're gonna keep in touch. She's from California, too, and we might work on a science project together and enter it into the Science Expo in Los Angeles next summer."

"Great," Will said.

"Where's Marsha?" Mack asked.

"She's talking to one of the guests inside the cantina." Marsha had entered the restaurant an hour after Will had vacated the cabin. He'd bought her an iced tea, then excused himself and had waited outside, afraid if he sat with her, he'd beg her to reconsider his marriage proposal.

"Ryan, why don't you tell your mom we're ready to go," Will said.

The teen ran off then stopped suddenly. "Thanks, Uncle Mack."

"From now on call me Mr. Cupid." Mack grinned.

When Ryan was out of earshot, Will said, "Thanks for making the afternoon special for him."

"Don't leave me hanging. Did Marsha accept your proposal?"

"No."

Mack winced. "What happened?"

"I don't want to talk about it." Will wanted to open

up to his brother, but he held everything inside, because he still hadn't digested all that had happened.

When Ryan and Marsha walked out of the cantina, Will said, "Thanks again for the invite today. Ryan hasn't been this excited all summer. I owe you one." He handed his brother the cabin key.

"Thank you, Mack," Marsha said, avoiding eye contact with Will. "Ryan had fun on the trail today."

"You two are welcome anytime." He clasped Ryan's shoulder. "Thank you for entertaining Amanda. She was bored to death until you showed up."

Ryan's cheeks reddened and Will came to his rescue. "We'd better get going."

Marsha and Ryan waved, then hopped into the pickup. As Will skirted the hood, Mack called out.

"You've got my number. Use it."

"If you've got time to waste talking to your brother then you need a girlfriend." Will hopped behind the wheel and shut the door on Mack's laughter. As he drove along the road to the highway, Will was grateful for Ryan's nonstop chatter about Amanda. As long as his son kept talking, he could ignore the tension between him and Marsha.

An hour later, Will turned onto the road leading to Pastor Bugler's home. The day couldn't end soon enough.

"Hey, Dad," Ryan said. "Can I spend the night at the farm? I want to work on the rocket. I told Amanda I'd post a Facebook photo of it."

"Honey, your father has things to do and—"

"Not really," Will said. Maybe Marsha didn't want to be with him, but his son did. "You're welcome to stay at the farm, Ryan." Will shifted into Park in the front driveway. "As a matter of fact, I'd like to show you the journal I've been keeping on my reading."

"Cool. I'll go pack my bag." Once Ryan went inside, Will and Marsha faced off.

"You don't have to do this," Marsha said.

"I enjoy being with Ryan."

"Will you bring him to work with you tomorrow morning?"

"That's up to him. He may want to sleep in past 5:00 a.m."

"I suppose I could drive out to the farm after I finish my tutoring session."

"Whatever works."

"When do you think you'll be done with the classroom wing?"

Why? Was she suddenly uncomfortable with him working under her nose? "Two weeks. Then Ben will do a walk-through with your father and they'll come up with a punch list of small fixes and we'll knock those out in a couple of days."

Will nodded. "Here comes Ryan." He saw a shadow in the doorway and assumed it was Marsha's father. He didn't care if the pastor wasn't happy that his grandson chose to be with his father—Marsha could deal with the man.

"Mind your manners, Ryan." She got out of the truck. "Bye, Mom."

Will smothered a smile behind a pretend cough when Ryan shut the door on Marsha before she'd given him a hug.

"Thanks for letting me stay the night, because I really need to talk to you about some stuff that I can't talk to Mom or Grandpa about."

"What kind of stuff?" he asked, driving off.

"Girl stuff."

"You and Amanda really hit it off, huh?"

"She's smart and super cool."

Maybe his son would have better luck with his lady love than Will was having with Marsha.

"I've never had a girlfriend before," Ryan said.

"You're young. You've got plenty of time for girls if you'd rather focus on school."

"How old were you when you got your first girlfriend?"

Will kept a straight face and said, "Eight. Her name was Jenny and the sun rose and set on her red braids and freckled face."

Ryan laughed. "Why'd you like her?"

"She shoved a boy on the playground after the kid made fun of my name."

"Kids teased you when you were little?"

"Willie Nelson Cash is a name that draws a lot of attention." He grinned. "I thought Jenny was the bravest girl in the world when she stood up to that bully."

"Did the bully push her?"

"Nope, he peed his pants and ran off. It was true love until the next recess and Jenny decided she liked Brent Dillinger better, because he could throw a baseball farther than me."

"When did you get your first serious crush?"

Will wasn't sure how to answer his son. "I dated a lot of girls on and off in high school, but there was never one I really fell hard for." *Except your mother, and I didn't know that until it was too late.*

"Did you…never mind."

"We haven't known each other long, but I hope you know you can always be open with me. The guy stuff we talk about stays between you and me," Will said.

"You won't tell my mom?"

"Nope. Not unless you ask me to intervene on your behalf."

"How old are most kids when they have sex?"

Will choked on his spit and coughed.

"You won't tell Mom I asked that question, will you?"

"No. Before I answer…have you kissed Amanda?"

"Amanda kissed me when Uncle Mack let us rest while he took the horses to get a drink."

How thoughtful of Mack to give teenagers with raging hormones privacy. "Was that your first kiss?"

"Yeah." Ryan blushed. "It was awesome."

Will chuckled. "First kisses usually are pretty awesome." He cleared his throat. "Take things slow with Amanda. If it's meant to be between you two it will work out."

If only Will could take his own advice, but Marsha hadn't given him a bit of hope that things would work out for them.

# Chapter Fourteen

Two weeks had passed since Will had taken Marsha and Ryan to the Black Jack Mountain Dude Ranch. She'd managed to avoid Will during the week but not on Sunday mornings when he showed up for church services and took a seat next to her and Ryan in the pew. Her father had grudgingly accepted Will's presence in his church as well as Ryan going with Will to the farm to work on the rocket.

"Where's Ryan?"

Marsha glanced up from her computer. Her father stood in the doorway. "He should be home in an hour."

Her father crossed the room and sat in the chair. Dark shadows ringed his eyes.

"Insomnia?"

He nodded.

"Why don't you lie down and take a short nap?" She felt helpless when it came to her father's health. No amount of praying would cure her father's cancer but it was all that was left in her father's arsenal of weapons after he stopped seeing his doctor.

"Too tired to sleep," he grumbled.

"What's Mom up to?"

"She's in Yuma having supper with Harriet Preston."

"That's right. She told me earlier she was spending the afternoon with her friend." His expression darkened. "Dad, are you in pain?"

"No more than the usual aches."

"Ever since you learned that Will fathered Ryan, the worry lines on your forehead have deepened." She offered a half smile, hoping to tease him into a good mood.

"I'm an old man and set in my ways. Takes me longer to adjust to change."

"You could buy more time and start cancer treatments again." The last thing she wanted to do was make her father feel guilty, but the desperate little girl inside her wasn't ready to let him go.

"Don't think I haven't struggled with my decision to allow nature to take its course."

This was the first time since she'd returned home that he'd opened the door to the subject and she jumped at the opportunity to share her feelings. "I know you have, Dad." Eyes smarting, she searched her heart for the right words. "I don't know what I'm going to do when you're gone." She sniffed. "You've been the only male in my life besides Ryan and you're my rock."

His eyes glistened with moisture when he looked at her. "You'll find the right man one day."

She'd already found the right man, but her father didn't approve of him. Not that it mattered—she'd messed things up with Will so badly he'd never give her a second chance.

She loved Will—so why had she lied to him at the dude ranch?

Her father cleared his throat. "William and Ryan appear to be getting along well."

"They are." Marsha couldn't be more pleased with how the father-son relationship was progressing.

"What do they do besides work on the rocket together?"

That her son hadn't mentioned Will's dyslexia told Marsha that he'd picked up on his grandfather's negative attitude toward Will. She hoped it wasn't so, but kids understood a lot more than adults gave them credit for.

"Ryan enjoys hanging out with the twins and their dog," she said. "They have fun swimming in the pond." And she had a sneaking suspicion that Will didn't ask many questions when Ryan chatted with his new girlfriend Amanda on Facebook.

"My grandson should be spending his energy on more productive—"

"Dad, Ryan pushes himself academically all year. There's no reason he can't relax and be a normal teenager during the summer."

Her father's finger tapped the chair's armrest. It was obvious he was struggling to come to terms with being forced to share his grandson with Will. "Ryan and William could hang out here."

Shocked by the suggestion, she said, "What do you mean?"

"They could play chess on the patio."

Marsha suspected her father was searching for a way to keep an eye on Will more than wanting to get to know him better. She stared into space, trying to envision Will, Ryan and her father sitting at a table playing a board game.

"Marsha."

Startled, she jerked in her chair.

"You've been distracted lately. What's wrong?"

He always could see through her.

"I'm a good listener," he said.

Her first instinct was to flee, but she stopped herself. For years she'd kept her feelings buried inside her. Maybe it was time—especially in light of her father's health—to settle the past. "You won't like what I have to say."

"Confession is good for the soul. Besides, I won't judge you."

Yes, he would judge her and be disappointed in her. Even though her mother was out of the house, Marsha got up from her chair and closed the office door—uncertain whether she was preventing herself or her father from escaping. She returned to the desk and considered her words carefully. She wouldn't go into the details, but she needed her father to know that the one time she and Will had been together he hadn't pushed her into doing anything she hadn't wanted to do.

"Dad, Will didn't pressure me to have sex the night of the prom. I initiated things between us."

As soon as the confession was out, Marsha's mind flashed back to the cabin at the dude ranch. Will had gotten it wrong. He believed she didn't love him and he couldn't be more mistaken. She'd loved Will forever. That love might have been born out of a teenage infatuation and a sexual encounter in the backseat of a truck, but her love for Will had grown deeper each year Ryan had celebrated a birthday.

"I don't understand." Her father stared at the wall, his face reddening with embarrassment. He was out of his comfort zone.

"I had a crush on Will my senior year but he wasn't interested in dating me. He barely knew I existed."

Who would have guessed the pastor's daughter had possessed the courage to pursue the school's notorious bad boy? "Buck set up the prom date with him for me." She'd begged for Buck's help, because she believed she wouldn't have an opportunity to be with Will once she left for college.

"Are you telling me that you were never alone with Will until the night of the prom?" he asked.

"That's right. I knew you wouldn't allow me to date him."

"You're right. I would not have allowed you anywhere near a Cash boy."

"Will didn't want the baby." *Or me.* "He wanted me to get an abortion."

"He abandoned you."

"I don't see it as abandonment, Dad. He wasn't ready to be a father any more than I was ready to be a mother."

"I'll agree with that," he said. "Why didn't you have an abortion? Your mother and I would never have known."

"Partly because of my faith and partly…" The truth was painful. "I saw my baby as a way to tie Will to me forever." If she couldn't have Will for herself, she could remain close to him through Ryan.

"But I don't understand why you went off to California without telling us you were pregnant."

"I knew you and Mom were going to be disappointed in me when you found out what I'd done, and I wanted to try and make it up to you by showing you that I could handle the responsibility of raising Ryan and going to college on my own. You expected me to earn a degree and I was determined not to fail you." In truth, she didn't think she could stand to see the look of disappointment in her father's eyes if she'd lived at home during her pregnancy.

"And I worried that if you knew I was pregnant, Mom would insist I live in Stagecoach and raise the baby here." And Marsha would have disappointed her father all over again when she didn't take advantage of the college scholarship she'd been offered.

"You could have come home after you'd earned your degree," he said.

Guilt had been the driving force behind Marsha's push to stay in school. "I knew you wanted me to pursue a higher degree. It was easier to earn my master's and doctorate at the university in California."

Her father's penetrating stare made Marsha nervous and she wished she knew what was going though his mind.

"Do you enjoy teaching?" he asked. "Is that what you've always wanted to do?"

"I love being in the classroom."

His eyes narrowed. "But…?"

*Don't back away from the truth now.* "My preference is to teach middle school," she said.

"Then why are you focusing on landing a college position?"

"Because I'm trying to make up for disappointing you and Mom."

Her father's eyes widened then the muscles in his face sagged. "You've been a fool, daughter."

She gasped.

"I forgave you for getting pregnant out of wedlock before your mother and I left your apartment in California after we first saw Ryan."

"You did?"

"Of course I did. You're my daughter. I love you, faults and all. Nothing you do or say will change that. I'm sorry we didn't have this talk years ago." His expression sobered. "Are you ready to forgive yourself?"

She'd believed the motivation and justification for her actions were tied to winning her parents' forgiveness when the real reason had been connected to her own guilt.

"You have some thinking to do, daughter." He walked out the door.

Tears flooded her eyes and she buried her face in her hands. She was grateful for her father's forgiveness, but it did little to ease her heartache. Had she been punishing herself all these years because she'd felt guilty for disappointing him? Her suffering was well-deserved but how could she have made Will and Ryan pay for her guilty feelings, too?

She had to speak with Will, but feared their chat wouldn't end as well as her talk with her father.

"THAT'S IT FOR THE PUNCH LIST," Ben said Friday morning.

Will ignored the empty feeling in his gut. As much as he hadn't appreciated Pastor Bugler looking over his shoulder these past weeks, he'd miss catching glimpses of Marsha coming and going each day while he worked.

"You want to grab a beer in town and celebrate?" Ben asked.

Will was about to accept the invite when Marsha stepped outside the house and walked in his direction.

"Looks like you might get a better offer." Ben chuckled. "If you change your mind, I'll be at Gilly's Tap House."

"Sure." Will stared at Marsha, glad he wore mirrored sunglasses, lest she see in his eyes how much he missed her. Loved her.

"Will." She stopped a few feet from him and offered a shy smile.

"Marsha." She looked hot in her neon-pink T-shirt and white jean shorts.

"Dad said you and Ben finished the punch list." She waved when Ben honked and drove off.

"We did." Will fisted his hands to keep from pulling her into his arms and begging her to give him…them a second chance. He'd hoped attending church service every Sunday would win him some points with the pastor but Marsha's father had treated him like every other parishioner and at the end of the service he shook Will's hand and thanked him for coming.

"Dad moved up the ribbon-cutting ceremony to this Sunday following the service," she said.

He didn't care about the ceremony and he sensed Marsha was beating around the bush. "What's Ryan doing?"

"He went with my mother to a movie at the mall in Yuma." She scuffed the toe of her sandal in the dirt. "Are you in a hurry, or can we talk?"

Will's heart tripped over itself. Had she changed her mind about his marriage proposal? "You want to take a drive?" he asked.

"That would be great." Without hesitation she opened the passenger door and hopped into the truck.

He started the engine then flipped on the air. Once the cab cooled, he drove out of the church parking lot. "Hungry?"

"Not really. If you are, feel free to stop and eat."

His stomach was too knotted for food. He drove west then turned off the main highway.

"Where does this road lead?" she asked.

"It ends at Lookout Rock."

"I've always wanted to see that place."

"You've never been out here?" Every kid he knew in high school had partied at the rock at least once.

"If word had ever spread that the pastor's daughter was seen at Lookout Rock, I'd have been grounded forever."

When they arrived at the rock, he parked, but kept the engine running. The dashboard thermometer read 101. "It's a little hot to hike to the top," he said. "But the views are decent from here."

"Is that the border with Mexico?" She pointed out the windshield.

"It's fifty miles past the horizon." All this small talk made him nervous and he wished she'd speak her mind. "Spit it out, Marsha."

"I lied to you."

His stomach clenched. "There's someone else?"

"It's always been you, Will."

"What do you mean?"

"I've loved you forever."

He didn't understand.

"In high school I had a crush on you and your bad-boy image. All I dreamed about was hopping on your Harley and the two of us taking off together."

Will didn't know where she was headed with her confession and kept quiet.

"Until Ryan was born I wasn't sure if what I felt in my heart for you was real love or infatuation. Once I held Ryan in my arms and saw your image in his face,

I knew I loved you." She waved a hand in the air. "But none of that matters."

His heart thudded painfully inside his chest.

"When you proposed at the dude ranch I gave you my reasons why it wouldn't be good for us to marry, but I wasn't being honest with you."

Will waited for her to continue, afraid to hope.

"I had a talk with my father and he confessed that he'd forgiven me years ago for becoming pregnant out of wedlock and hiding your identity from him." Her eyes watered. "His admission forced me to face the truth— that in my heart I did know that my father had forgiven me, but I ignored the knowledge, because it was easier to live with blaming him than myself for things not working out between you and me."

"I don't understand," Will said.

"I never told you about Ryan because I was afraid you'd reject me."

"Reject you how?"

"After I confessed I was pregnant and you insisted I get an abortion, I realized that a guy like you could never love a girl like me. I thought if I kept Ryan a secret I wouldn't have to face the fact that you didn't love me."

This was a lot for Will to take in. "You made a decision that changed both of our lives forever." He thought of the night he'd proposed to Rachel then afterward had dreamed of Marsha. "I need some air."

Will got out of the pickup and walked a few yards away, then stopped and stared into the desert. The midday sun beat down on his head but the burn did little to ease the cold chill seeping into his bones.

He wouldn't be human if he didn't admit that he was thrilled Marsha had loved him since high school, but her love had been wasted on him—he'd been in no shape to return it. If she'd told him she'd kept the baby they would have ended up together—because her father would have pressured them to marry and he would have grown to resent Marsha. In all probability they'd be divorced by now.

He heard the truck door open and close behind him. He faced her and the look of despair in her eyes cut him to the core. "You shouldn't have kept Ryan a secret from me."

"I know. Can you forgive me?"

That was the easy part. "Yes."

"Promise me you won't hold what I've done against Ryan," she said.

How could she think he'd do that? "I'll always worry about my ability to be a good father. I'll second-guess myself a lot over the next few decades, but I'm not running from the responsibility."

Marsha had been truthful with him—he owed her the same courtesy. "When I was a kid I bugged my mother with questions about my father and one day she gave in and took me to his house in Tucson."

"What happened?"

"I found out he was married and had kids younger than me."

"What did he say to you?"

"He told me to get lost."

She gasped. "I'm sorry, Will."

"My father's rejection did a number on me. I thought there was something wrong with me if he couldn't love me. Add that to my dyslexia and I admit to having my share of insecurities. When you became pregnant, my first thought was that I wasn't good enough to be our baby's father." He shrugged. "Then when you sent that letter telling me about Ryan—"

"You thought I had kept him a secret because *I* didn't believe you were good enough to be his father."

He nodded. "And when I learned how smart Ryan was, I figured I didn't stand a chance with him. I could live with your father believing I wasn't good enough for his grandson, but I couldn't live with my own son looking down his nose at me."

"Where do we go from here?" Marsha's voice cracked.

Will knew she was asking him if he would give her a second chance, but he couldn't ignore the strong bond between the pastor and his daughter. He'd yearned for that same bond with his old man and refused to make Marsha choose between pleasing her father and being with him—no matter how much he loved her.

"We keep moving forward. Take it one a day at a time."

Her eyes widened, then she nodded and got back into the truck and they drove in silence to the church.

When he parked in front of her parents' house, she said, "You're invited to stay after the service this Sunday for the ribbon-cutting ceremony."

That was a special day for the pastor and his church. Will would attend the service but not the celebration. He didn't want his presence to put a damper on the party. "Tell Ryan to give me a call. I thought maybe I'd take him to tour the Biosphere 2 north of Tucson."

"He'd like that." Marsha shut the door and marched up the sidewalk determined to get into the house before she broke down. She hadn't made it through the living room when her father blocked her path.

"What's the matter?" His mouth turned down when he saw the tears in her eyes.

"I did what you said. I told Will the truth about why I kept Ryan a secret from him."

"Did he forgive you?"

"Of course he did."

"Did you tell him that you love him?"

"Yes."

"And…"

"He said we'll take it one day at a time."

"Why would he say that?"

"Because he knows you don't approve of him."

"Since when does a man like William Cash care what others thinks of him?"

"Since he knows how important your approval is to me and he's too good of a man to make me choose between the two of you." Marsha had to leave the room before she broke down. God help her, this was turning out to be the most emotional summer of her life and all bets were off as to whether or not she'd survive it.

WILL STEPPED OUTSIDE the bunkhouse late Saturday afternoon and stared at the sky. A wall of dark clouds worked its way toward the farm. Conway was tinkering with the tractor in the barn, so he hurried to the farmhouse to find out if Isi had seen a weather forecast on TV.

She opened the back door before he made it to the steps. "The weather alert went off, Will."

"Are the boys inside with you?"

Isi stared over Will's shoulder and he turned. Conway strode toward him, a grim expression on his face. "This one looks bad," he said.

Will climbed the porch steps with his brother. "Have you heard from Porter today?"

"Mack asked Porter to fill in this weekend for a sick employee at the dude ranch," Conway said. "I think the storm will miss them, but Stagecoach is in its path."

"I'll text Shannon and make sure she knows, in case Johnny's out with the cattle," Will said. First, he'd text Ryan. He had no idea if his son was running errands with his mother or sitting in his grandparents' home reading a book on his e-reader, unaware of the approaching storm. He hoped the church or the pastor's home had a storm shelter.

While waiting to hear from Ryan, Will texted Shannon and Dixie and they confirmed that they were aware of the storm and taking shelter. Ryan finally texted Will that he and his mother and grandparents were hiding in a hall closet in the house. Will wished he was with Ryan and Marsha, but the storm was moving fast and he had no time to drive to the church.

Conway and Isi came outside with the twins and Bandit, who had been put on a leash. "Here." Conway handed Will a sack of supplies and a jug of water. "We're waiting this one out in Grandma's cellar." Conway picked up both boys and hustled toward the barn, Isi followed with Bandit, who zigzagged in front of her, spooked by the storm. As the group cut across the yard, a big gust of wind almost knocked Isi down and Will wrapped an arm around her waist to steady her.

Conway set the boys down inside the barn and opened a door in the dirt floor.

"Do I have to go down there?" Miguel asked. "It's dark."

The twins hovered close to Isi and Will didn't blame

them for being scared. "I'll go first and light the lantern." Will descended the steps, found the battery-operated lantern and flipped it on. After making sure there were no rodents in residence he said, "Coast is clear." Will guided the boys into the shelter. "You two sit on the bench." Isi came down next then Bandit and Conway, who shut the door behind him.

A loud crack of thunder startled the twins and they jumped off the bench and cowered against Conway's legs. Bandit whined like a big baby.

Will thought of Ryan and Marsha. The need to keep them safe was so strong it startled him. He'd only met his son a short while ago yet learning he was Ryan's father had been all he'd needed for his parental instincts to kick in and feel protective of the teen. Will considered his own father and how easily the man had brushed him off. Will's developing relationship with Ryan proved he was nothing like his old man.

A loud crash exploded above their heads and the boys yelped.

"There go my tools," Conway said.

"I don't like storms," Javi said.

Conway hugged the twins. "It'll be over in a few minutes, guys."

"I hope the house is still standing," Isi said.

Another loud thud sounded and Will pictured half the barn gone when they emerged from the shelter. After ten minutes, the whistling wind stopped. Conway waited another minute then climbed the steps and opened the door. "The storm passed." He stepped from the cellar then helped Isi out. The boys went next then Will turned off the lantern and came up with the dog, shutting the door behind him.

The inside of the barn was a disaster. More than half the wood slats on the south side of the structure were missing. The yard was littered with tools.

"Watch Bandit," Conway said. "We don't want him to step on any broken glass or twisted metal."

The group picked their way across the debris. "The house looks in good shape." Will noted a few roof shingles lay on the ground.

The yard was a mess, but the pecan groves appeared to have weathered the storm well and Will didn't see any uprooted trees. Bandit's doghouse, on the other hand, had flown across the yard and was jammed beneath the front bumper of Conway's black Dodge.

Will glanced over his shoulder at the bunkhouse. Debris had slammed into the sides, denting the metal, but it remained in one piece, as did the satellite dish.

"Your truck door's dented, Will," Conway said.

Not only dented, but whatever hit the panel had scratched the paint off. "Insurance will cover that."

"I'll put the coffee on," Isi said. "We're going to lose daylight soon." The boys trailed their mother into the house, Bandit on their heels.

While Conway examined the barn wall, Will texted Ryan for an update and was relieved when his son confirmed that they were fine. The next text had Will cursing.

"What's the matter?" Conway asked.

"Ryan said the storm left a big hole in the church roof and the parking lot is filled with tree branches." He glanced at his phone again. "He said the new classroom wing is fine, only a couple of broken windows."

"That's a relief."

"The ribbon-cutting ceremony for the new wing is tomorrow." Will stared at his brother.

Conway groaned. "You're not thinking what I think you're thinking, are you?"

Will nodded.

"If I help you clean up the church, does that mean we call it even?"

After Will had faked an interest in Isi to make Conway jealous, which resulted in Conway gathering the courage to ask Isi to marry him, Will had demanded he be able to call in a future favor for his matchmaking help. "Deal."

"We'd better contact every cowboy we know," Will said. "It's going to take more than me and you to get the church cleaned up before the morning service."

"DAD?" MARSHA STEPPED into her father's office at the crack of dawn Sunday morning. The lines across his forehead appeared deeper and his skin paler—he probably hadn't slept a wink last night, worrying about repairs that needed to be done to the church. "What's all that racket outside?"

He moved away from the window. "See for yourself."

She sucked in a quiet breath. The church parking lot was filled with cowboys and Will stood in the middle of the group giving out orders. She spotted Ben Wallace and his brother in the mix, as well as Will's brothers Johnny, Conway, Porter, Mack and their brother-in-law, Gavin.

After the group broke apart, chain saws began buzzing and within minutes a path had been cut across the road. As the men cleared the parking lot of debris, Will and Ben placed a ladder against the side of the church and Will climbed onto the roof.

Heart in her throat, Marsha watched Will examine the gaping hole, praying he wouldn't lose his balance and fall through it. Porter carried a roll of tar paper up the ladder, then reached behind him and took the package of roof shingles from Conway and handed those off to Will. Will stood and Marsha felt her face grow warm as her gaze travelled over him. Did he have any idea how sexy he looked in his cowboy hat, faded jeans and a tool belt slung low on his hips?

"Mom?" Ryan stumbled into the room along with her mother.

"The cavalry has arrived," she said.

Ryan squeezed between her and his grandfather. "Is that Dad on the church roof?" he asked.

Marsha's heart melted at the note of affection she heard in Ryan's voice. No matter what happened between her and Will, her son would always have a father. Speaking of fathers…the pastor was studying her. Their gazes clashed, then a moment later he gave a firm nod and disappeared.

Marsha rubbed Ryan's back. "C'mon, sleepyhead, let's go outside and see what we can do to help."

"I'll put on the coffee and start making pancakes," her mother said as she passed by the office door.

Marsha raced down the hall to her bedroom and slipped on a pair of jeans and an old T-shirt before putting on her athletic shoes. Ryan met her at the door, dressed in shorts and a T-shirt. Halfway across the parking lot Marsha heard her father raise his voice.

"William Cash!"

The chain saws stopped rumbling and the men stared at Marsha's father.

Will looked over his shoulder. "Yes, sir."

"I was wrong about you," her father said.

"Is that so?"

"Do you love my daughter?"

Will's gaze shifted to Marsha. "Yes, sir, I do."

"And you'll take your duty as Ryan's father seriously?"

"I will."

Her father faced the crowd of workers. "Get busy and clean this place up. We've got a wedding to prepare for today!"

"Mom." Ryan tugged her arm. "Are you and Dad getting married?"

"Yes, they are," her father answered for Marsha. He glanced between her and Ryan. "Daughter, you won't find a better man than William Cash to stand by your side and share your life with. And Ryan, you won't find a better father to support your goals and to be there to give you advice than the man working on my church roof."

"I know, Grandpa," Ryan said. "My dad's a lot smarter than you think."

Marsha heard a chuckle behind her.

Johnny Cash grinned. "And Ryan's got plenty of uncles who'll be happy to lend advice or a helping hand as he grows up."

Her father pointed his finger. "I'm counting on you, Johnny, to keep Ryan's uncles in line...or else."

Johnny nodded. "You think you can squeeze in a double baptism before the wedding?"

Her father's face lit up with joy. "Make sure those babies are here by noon."

Marsha's eyes welled with tears—Johnny had extended an olive branch to her father.

"I'm going inside to tell Grandma you're marrying Dad." Ryan took off.

"Pastor Bugler, I need you to take a look at…"

After Marsha's father walked away with Ben, she went over to the ladder leaning against the church and stared up at Will. The man had no right to look that sexy standing on the roof of a church. "Will…if you feel like you've been pressured into—"

He descended the ladder, then took her hands in his. "I don't know what changed your father's opinion of me, but I don't hold grudges. He's given us his blessing and I want to spend the rest of my days with you and Ryan." Will lowered his face to hers. "I love you, Marsha. I'm ready to make a commitment to you and Ryan today in your father's church."

Marsha leaned into Will and kissed him, ignoring the hoots and hollers of his brothers and friends. When the kiss ended, she said, "We have a lot to figure out. Where we'll live…our jobs and—"

"It's not complicated, honey." He kissed her long and hard. "Wherever you are…there I am."

FIVE HOURS LATER the parking lot had been cleared of debris and the church was packed with parishioners and the cowboys who'd helped clean up after the storm. Marsha, Will and Ryan sat at the front of the church along with the rest of the Cash brothers—except Buck. Marsha's heart ached that her returning home to Stagecoach had caused a rift between Will and Buck. She vowed that after the hoopla from the wedding died down, she'd talk to Will and see if he could persuade Buck to return to the farm.

A squawk next to Marsha brought a smile to her face. Johnny and Shannon had arrived a half hour ago with little Addy, and Dixie and Gavin had shown up with their son, Nathan, shortly after. It had been ages since her father had performed a baptism and she suspected that and not her wedding would be the highlight of his day.

Heads bowed, and her father gave the opening prayer then invited Marsha's mother up to the pulpit where she introduced Johnny and his wife then Dixie and her husband. The two couples and their babies joined Marsha's parents in front of the congregation.

As her father anointed each baby's head, Marsha noticed the sparkle that had been missing from his eyes was back. Maybe now he'd change his mind and talk to his doctor about fighting his cancer—today showed that he had a lot to live for.

Once the baptisms were completed and the proud parents sat in the pews again, her father said, "I now have the honor of marrying my daughter to a man I couldn't be prouder to call my son."

"You ready?" Will whispered.

She spoke from the heart. "I've been ready since prom night."

The ceremony was short but poignant. They stood before her father and God—Marsha in her yellow sundress and Will in jeans and a white dress shirt.

When her father pronounced them husband and wife, Marsha expected a demure kiss from her new husband. Instead, he bent her over his knee and planted a lusty smooch on her mouth. The cowboys whistled and applauded.

After Will let her come up for air, he winked at her father. "You didn't think I'd given up *all* my wild ways, did you?"

Her father's chuckle echoed through the church as Marsha and Will strolled down the aisle. When they passed Ryan, she reached for his hand and together the three of them left the church as the family they were always meant to be.

\* \* \* \* \*

*Find out who steals Buck's heart in the next*
CASH BROTHERS *novel by Marin Thomas!*
*Available in May 2014 wherever*
*Harlequin American Romance books are sold.*

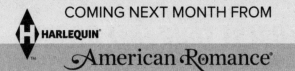
Available March 4, 2014

## #1489 THE TEXAS WILDCATTER'S BABY
*McCabe Homecoming*
by Cathy Gillen Thacker

Environmentalist Rand McCabe embarks on a passionate affair with lady wildcatter Ginger Rollins, but can't convince her to begin a real relationship with him...until she finds herself unexpectedly pregnant with his child.

## #1490 MOST ELIGIBLE SHERIFF
*Sweetheart, Nevada*
by Cathy McDavid

Ruby McPhee switches places with her twin sister so she can lay low in Sweetheart, Nevada. She doesn't expect complications—except it turns out Ruby is "dating" Cliff Dempsey, local sheriff and the town's most eligible bachelor!

## #1491 AIMING FOR THE COWBOY
*Fatherhood*
by Mary Leo

An unexpected pregnancy hog-ties Helen Shaw's rodeo career and friendship with future father Colt Granger. The sexy cowboy's proposal sounds sweet, but is it the real deal?

## #1492 ROPING THE RANCHER
by Julie Benson

Colt Montgomery has sworn off women after his ex left him to raise his teenage daughter alone. When actress Stacy Michaels shows up at his ranch, she tests his resolve to steer clear of women!

---

# REQUEST YOUR FREE BOOKS!
## 2 FREE NOVELS PLUS 2 FREE GIFTS!

**HARLEQUIN**®

*American ★ Romance*®

## LOVE, HOME & HAPPINESS

**YES!** Please send me 2 FREE Harlequin® American Romance® novels and my 2 FREE gifts (gifts are worth about $10). After receiving them, if I don't wish to receive any more books, I can return the shipping statement marked "cancel." If I don't cancel, I will receive 4 brand-new novels every month and be billed just $4.74 per book in the U.S. or $5.24 per book in Canada. That's a savings of at least 14% off the cover price! It's quite a bargain! Shipping and handling is just 50¢ per book in the U.S. and 75¢ per book in Canada.* I understand that accepting the 2 free books and gifts places me under no obligation to buy anything. I can always return a shipment and cancel at any time. Even if I never buy another book, the two free books and gifts are mine to keep forever.

154/354 HDN F4YN

Name _____ (PLEASE PRINT) _____

Address _____ Apt. # _____

City _____ State/Prov. _____ Zip/Postal Code _____

Signature (if under 18, a parent or guardian must sign) _____

Mail to the **Harlequin**® **Reader Service:**
**IN U.S.A.:** P.O. Box 1867, Buffalo, NY 14240-1867
**IN CANADA:** P.O. Box 609, Fort Erie, Ontario L2A 5X3

**Want to try two free books from another line?**
**Call 1-800-873-8635 or visit www.ReaderService.com.**

\* Terms and prices subject to change without notice. Prices do not include applicable taxes. Sales tax applicable in N.Y. Canadian residents will be charged applicable taxes. Offer not valid in Quebec. This offer is limited to one order per household. Not valid for current subscribers to Harlequin American Romance books. All orders subject to credit approval. Credit or debit balances in a customer's account(s) may be offset by any other outstanding balance owed by or to the customer. Please allow 4 to 6 weeks for delivery. Offer available while quantities last.

**Your Privacy**—The Harlequin® Reader Service is committed to protecting your privacy. Our Privacy Policy is available online at www.ReaderService.com or upon request from the Harlequin Reader Service.

We make a portion of our mailing list available to reputable third parties that offer products we believe may interest you. If you prefer that we not exchange your name with third parties, or if you wish to clarify or modify your communication preferences, please visit us at www.ReaderService.com/consumerchoice or write to us at Harlequin Reader Service Preference Service, P.O. Box 9062, Buffalo, NY 14269. Include your complete name and address.

HARI3R

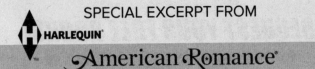
Picking up the bouquet, Cliff said, "These are for you."

"Thanks." Scarlett accepted the flowers and, with both
hands full, set them back down on the table. "You didn't have
to."

"They're a bribe. I was hoping you'd go with me to the
square dance Friday night."

The community center had finally reopened nearly a year
after the fire. The barbecue and dance were in celebration.

"I…um…don't think I can. I appreciate the invitation
though."

"Are you going with someone else?" He didn't like the
idea of that.

"No, no. I'm just…busy." She clutched her mug tightly
between both hands.

"I'd really like to take you." Fifteen minutes ago he probably
wouldn't have put up a fight and would have accepted her loss
of interest. Except he was suddenly more interested in her
than before. "Think on it overnight."

"O-kay." She took another sip of her coffee. As she did, the
cuff of her shirtsleeve pulled back.

He saw it then, a small tattoo on the inside of her left wrist.

esembling a shooting star. A jolt coursed through him. He hadn't seen the tattoo before.

Because seven days ago, when he and Scarlett ate dinner at the I Do Café, it hadn't been there.

"Is that new?" He pointed to the tattoo.

Panic filled her eyes. "Um…yeah. It is."

Cliff didn't buy her story. There were no tattoo parlors in Sweetheart and, to his knowledge, she hadn't left town. And why the sudden panic?

Scarlett averted her face. She was hiding something.

Leaning down, he smelled her hair, which reminded him of the flowers he'd brought for her. It wasn't at all how Scarlett normally smelled.

Something was seriously wrong.

He scrutinized her face. Eyes, chocolate-brown and fathomless. Same as before. Hair, thick and glossy as mink's fur. Her lips, however, were different. More ripe, more lush and incredibly kissable.

He didn't stop to think and simply reacted. The next instant, his mouth covered hers.

She squirmed and squealed and wrestled him. Hot coffee splashed onto his chest and down his slacks. He let her go, but not because of any pain.

"Are you crazy?" she demanded, her breath coming fast.

Holding on to the wrist with the new tattoo, he narrowed his gaze. "Who the hell are you? And don't bother lying, because I know you aren't Scarlett McPhee."

*Look for* MOST ELIGIBLE SHERIFF *by Cathy McDavid next month from Harlequin® American Romance®!*